COUNTRY BOY

The Rise and Fall of A Southern Legend

Alan Little

Play
MULTIMEDIA AND PUBLISHING

Chapter One

Country Boys

It all started Friday morning, business as usual.

"Damn this fuckin' two-way is driving me nuts. 919-997-2318. Yo' did someone hit me from this number?"

A silky voice answers. "It's all according to who I'm speaking to."

"Look Shorty, it's too early for games."

"Oh yeah, well is it too early for Champagne?"

Just hearing that name makes his body respond and his mind begin to think back. Champagne is a stripper named Asia that he had met at The Crew's club. All of his boys are big up on the dancers from out of town. Corey and Poo handle most of the shows and business dealings at the club. They allow the girls to come from different strip-joints from around Charlotte and Fayetteville, N.C. The girls hang in the back office with the rest of The Crew while they play poker. Whoever wins a hand, will tip their favorite stripper, who is usually already clinging to their neck.

Q is never too big on the stripper thing, so some of the girls who push up on him, feel like he is being all stuck up and shit. Fact is, he knows why and what they are there for, the money and street glory that he has. He just comes to watch the spade game and recuperate from a long day.

One night, Tim places a call to his cell and informs him about one of the girls that his cousin brought in, who has been dancing for about two weeks and shows interest in him. "The new girl done heard about you fam, and wants to meet you... You want me to set that up?" Tim questions

"Nah, homie, you know what's up when it comes to that. I'm focused on making money, not trickin' off. Ain't nuttin' happening with that."

"Aight big homie, I got it. Just relaying the message, that's it."

"Good looking out tho'. I'll get at you later tonight at the club," Q replies.

The line at the club is all the way back to Main Street. Big Kev sees Q's black 740 iL, creeping past the line of cars waiting to be searched for weapons. He sticks his flashlight out and signals Q around the line of cars.

"Damn, that nigga got this whole side of town on lock," says a local hustler named Tech. "Look at the way mothafuckas bowing down to this nigga," Tech adds.

"Yea that's my nigga Q," says AJ.

"I don't care who he is, his ass can wait in line like everybody else," Tech states with animosity.

"Hold up, my nigga. Unless you tryin' to get yourself killed, please leave that shit alone. He ain't bothering us, and we ain't about to bother him."

"You act like that nigga's God or somebody."

"I didn't say that. He's not God, but he will have you standing in front of God before daybreak, if you think it's a game. Now get your ass ready to put that energy in the sound booth, before you have six of your closest homies carrying yo' black ass around the back of the church." AJ informs him.

"Yeah whatever, aight," Tech states, letting the conversation go, as they proceed about their business.

SHAE AND TAB ARE TWO GIRLS WORKING THE BOOTH AT THE VALET. They recognize Q's car and begin fixing their skimpy outfits.

"Damn Tab, there goes fine ass Q. That nigga so dark and lovely, he looks like he is made for that car," Shae fantasizes.

"Yeah girl, that nigga can always have pussy as long as I got one," Tab counters being honest.

Q pulls to the left side of the parking lot, where he is met by a valet attendant who immediately opens his door. He gets out, adjusts his clothes and walks toward the valet booth. With each step, people are whispering and greeting him so much, you would have thought Tyrese or somebody had gotten out of the car.

"Look at all these bitches sweating my man," says Tab.

"Yo' man, huh?" says Shae.

"Yeah bitch, he's my man tonight." Both girls laugh.

Q stops and speaks to a group of females standing near the booth. They all got into their killer stances, trying to gain an edge on the next chick. You know pigeon-toed, bow-legged, hands on the hip type shit.

"What up, Quentel?" a cutie by the name of Angie says. She knows she had to have known him well to be using his government name like that.

"What's good Angie, how's that beautiful little girl doing?"

"She's fine, spoiled rotten though."

Angie has a daughter named Lexus, who, like her, is gorgeous. Angie has these green eyes that would hypnotize a nigga. Q always knew she had a crazy crush on him, but he has only been with three light-skinned women in his life. He likes his meat dark.

Q hollers at Tab, "Yo Tab, let them in for free Baby-Girl, it's on me okay?"

"Aight Q. Now please go inside the club before you let everybody in for free," she says, eyeing the group of girls.

Once he enters the club, he can feel the eyes on him. This always makes him uneasy. Crowded places make Q feel claustrophobic and uncomfortable. He always wonders if they can read the nervousness from his body. He slides quickly to the back offices where his boys are. When he enters the room, he is greeted by all types of fragrances. The one thing about strippers is that they all smelled like some fruity lotion. The whole crew is around the poker table.

Q speaks, "What's up fellas, ladies? Man, it's packed out there. Cars backed up damn near a mile down the road and people still tryin' to get in this bitch." He points at Corey. "The fire code fine is $1500. Break that shit, and it's on you nigga."

"Nigga, it's all good. I paid the Fire Chief $350 to get the count fucked up, so we straight."

Suddenly, there is a loud knock at the door. Instinct made every nigga in the room reach for they shit. Suddenly a stripper named Cream yells, "Hold up y'all, it's probably my cousin Asia."

Tim opens the door. The female that walks through catches Q completely off guard. His first thought is that she can't be a stripper, even though she has the complete package; you know, light eyes, small waist, and from behind it looks like two lil' boys wrestling to get out of her pants. After the formal introductions, everyone can easily see that Asia has gotten more words out of Q than any stripper.

"So you're the famous Q, huh? I've heard so many things about you," Asia tells him.

"You shouldn't believe everything you hear."

"I didn't say that I believed anything. Besides, I'm the type who believes it when she sees it," she states seductively.

Q likes her sassiness. After a couple of quick glances and brief conversational exchanges, Q pulls her to his back office, and she begins to tell him her life story. He takes an immediate liking to Asia, who he learns is also a junior at Fayetteville State and a part-time secretary for a law firm. Q always has respect for women who work hard for what they want out of life. This is a quality most strippers, or women in general, didn't possess. Q quickly knows this is the type of female he wants and needs on his team.

"Yo, how about we get up out of here and find a better place to talk?"

"That's cool. Let me let my cousin know we about to bounce." As they begin to exit the club, Asia can feel the envious eyes on her. When they arrive at Q's car, he goes to her side and opens the door.

"Damn! A southern gentleman, huh?" Asia says surprised.

"Yo, you know how we do it down south. Plus, I want you to save those hands for later."

"And what will they be doing later?"

"I thought maybe you could give a brotha a massage or something."

"The massage, I'm alright with. It's the 'or something' I'm worried about," she replies innocently.

Q just smiles as he starts to drive to one of his spots he keeps around town. Any true playa knows he can't take a woman he just met to the place he lays his head, even though he is really feeling Asia.

When they arrive at the spot, Q walks Asia inside the apartment. She is immediately impressed. Though this is just a layover spot, Q has it laced out. Plasma TVs, leather, the whole nine.

"What type of music you like?" Q asks.

"Anything slow," she responds with a smile.

As R Kelly begins to sing, Q thinks it's a good time to take Asia up on the massage. "Ma, what's up with the massage we talked about?"

"Am I getting paid for this?" she asks jokingly.

"Yeah, whatever you want. Just make sure I'm not wasting my money."

"Oh, I do believe you'll get your money's worth," she says.

Q lays on the bed face down, eyes closed, while she begins to massage his body.

"Damn loosen up," Asia says to him. "Your back is so tense."

She notices how tight every dense muscle in his thick back is. She slowly eases down to his lower back. Q's body begins to react to her soft touch. She begins to rub the inner part of his thigh. That is all he can stand. He turns over and looks into her hazel eyes. It seems like she senses his thoughts and starts kissing his lips softly. They trade lip positions for what seems like an hour.

They exchange sexual escapades a couple more times, and then Q realizes it is getting late, and he needs to be heading home. Though he is definitely a man's man, truth be told, he has a curfew and time is winding down. After a quick wash up, he gives Asia his info and gets hers. They agree to see each other again. Soon after, he heads home.

The next morning, Q is awakened by the common smell he has grown accustomed to. The smell of bacon and eggs is all throughout the house. He lies awake with the covers pulled over his head, his mind drifting back to the wild and crazy night he just had. He comes out from under the covers and stares at the fan slowly moving above him on his mirrored ceiling. He is suddenly snapped out of his trance by the opening of his bedroom door. It is his girlfriend Tashonda, Tee for short. Tee is what every hustler dreams of. She stands 5'8" tall, with short cropped hair, nice big lips, small waist, and a fat ass. Their relationship, like most others, has its ups and downs, but their love for one another is unconditional.

"What's up with you, sexy?" Q says in a sleepy voice.

"No, what's up with you? You the one about to miss curfew last night," Tee responds with a raised eyebrow. "Must have been a long night at the club, the way you were sleeping."

"Yea, you know how niggas be acting. I didn't want to leave Tim there by himself." Q gives Tee the once over and lets her know he didn't approve of the tight dress she had on. "Where you going anyway?"

"To see my other man. Why?" Tee says jokingly.

"I know it ain't no nigga around here crazy enough to mess wit my shit."

"Yo shit? I thought this belonged to me."

"Use to. Now it's mine."

Tee laughs and tells him she is about to go shopping with her girls and heads toward the door.

"Come back here and give your nigga some love."

"Nah. You save that for tonight," she says as she heads out the door.

Q looks over at the clock and realizes it is time for him to start his day as well. After showering, he calls Tim for a check up on the block. "What's up, fam?"

"Nothing much, but we need to meet up. We might have a little trouble."

"Shit, I'm on my way nigga." Q throws on some jeans, a white T, and a fresh pair of Air One's and heads out the door. "Damn which one today? The car or the bike?"

Q decides the bike, just in case he needs to handle some business. Motorcycles are his passion. He loves the feel of being on a bike. Today, he chooses his pride and joy, a black Suzuki 1300 with chromed out wheels.

Q, Pooh, and Umar all lean on the seats of their Sukes. Ten minutes earlier, Fat Dave had text all three simultaneously on the hip with the "Code 45". All three know that means there is possible trouble on the block. They all enter from three different directions: one from Hood St., one from Armstead, and the other from Leak St. Now, they sit and listen to Fat Dave tell them about some new kid from D.C. questioning the young niggas about their leader.

Q sits quietly listening, lost in his own thoughts. It has only been three days since Tim mentioned those same words about some out of town cat wanting to meet him. Q lives by the old code "The fewer people you know the better!" But this cat is determined and that makes Q curious. Q stands up, unlocks his seat and puts his 44 magnum underneath it. He settles back down on the seat of his bike before he speaks for the first time. "I want to meet this nigga."

"What!" replies Umar.

"I says, I want to meet him. Either he's a real nigga or a dead nigga, it's that simple." With that said, the conversation is over and the men part ways.

Club Mercedes is once again the hottest spot in all the surrounding counties. It is located on I-77 South outside of Rockingham, North Carolina. Rockingham is also known as

'The Rock, The Racing Capital of The World'. The featured attraction for the night is a rap group called The Ying Yang Twins. Everyone would be in the house tonight. Security has to be tight. Gunplay could definitely be an issue.

"Kev, what time will security arrive?" Tim asks over his cellphone.

"They pulled up about ten minutes ago." Kev replies, while standing in the club.

"Good. Let Big Ant know what's up," Tim orders.

"Aight, but he's handing out flashlights and badges."

"Aight then, nigga. I'm about to hit Q and see if he wants to check The Block before we head to the club."

Kev closes his cellphone and peeps around the club. Big Ant's extra security will help keep the hostile crowd in check, at least he hoped it would.

Ballers from all over will be in the house: Charlotte, Greensboro, Fayetteville, Stoneville, Hamlet, Rockingham, and South Carolina. You name it, they'd be there. Dressed to impress with enough jewelry on to make Wells Fargo have to write a check. Add that with some USDA Prime Fat Bitches, half naked, and the ABC store behind the bar... You're bound to have some drama.

Tim's cell phone rings as he gives Q a call. "What up man?"

"It ain't nothing."

"Do you want me to scoop you up or meet you at the club?"

"Nah, Baby Boy, meet me on The Block at around 11:00." Beep-Beep.

"My phone's beeping so get at me then."

"Yeah."

Q switches over to the other line. "Yes?"

"What's up Q? This El, is Tee there with you? Her phone keeps going straight to voicemail."

"What up El? She right here."

El is short for Elbony. She is Tee's best friend. They are also both in their last semester at Chris Logan Beauty College. Tee has already rented the building for her future salon. She has bought almost everything, including three chairs. Elbony will be her partner.

"Yo, Tee, it's El," Q hollers as he tosses her the phone.

"What up, girl?" El asks.

"What's up? It's more like what's taking you so long! I been sittin' here waitin' on yo' ass."

"Wait a minute, slut. Last I remember, it takes somebody at least an extra hour to shave their hairy chest," El banters back.

"Funny, bitch. You probably just got off your stomach anyway."

"Nah bitch, my knees, and it is delicious," El says laughing. "You are so crazy girl."

"I'll be there at ten."

"Don't be late. You know them Ying Yang Twins will be in the house tonight, and that shit's probably already packed."

"Come on El, it's only 9:00, and you know we have our table up front, straight VIP, no waiting in line, nothing. So stop bitchin'."

"Aight ho," El agrees.

"Takes one to know one."

"Ten," El demands.

"Ten it is."

Q steps out of the shower just as Tee is calling his name.

"Yeah, what up ma."

"I'm on my way to get El and head to the club."

"Aight, be safe."

Q turns to the mirror on the wall to lotion up when he feels Tee's soft hands around his waist. She plants soft kisses down the center of his back until his whole body tenses up, easing her hand inside the towel he had wrapped around him. After Q's heart rate comes back down to normal, he sits on the edge of the bed and looks at his woman preparing to leave. She has on a thigh length Versace mini dress that displays every curve and detail of her body. Her well toned legs and manicured feet make a nigga's mouth water.

"See you in a little while," says Q.

"Don't be too long, baby," she responds. Tee is hip to the way crowded places make Q uncomfortable, so he will always show up as late as possible.

"I won't baby. I will see you in a minute."

It is 11:00 p.m. when Q pulls up on The Block. He sits in his drop top, 645 arctic blue BMW, scoping the scene. Money is booming. The Block consists of two hole-in-the-wall clubs. These spots took on the appearance of a candy store in the daytime, but by night, they are full fledged gambling spots. The Chill-Grill is the food spot. It is run by Mrs. Janie. All the corner hustlers eat there every day. She cooks 24-7. Rumor has it, she is just as rich and gangster as any baller on The Block. A crackhead tried to rob her once and ended up across the street in Nelson's Funeral Home with a .38 slug between the eyes. The white people respected her so much, she didn't even have to go downtown.

Q spots Tim across the street in front of Grady's Store. He slides his

.45 into its arm holster under his LRG Jacket before exiting his car. He eases between two parked cars and heads toward Tim, who is still having a conversation with two cats from around the block named Dirk and Camron.

"What up T?" says Q.

"Nothing homie. Gettin' this cheddar. Cam and Dee want half a bird, but they only got twelve five."

As much money as Cam and Dee have spent with Q, he didn't even think twice. "What you waitin' on nigga... Bless them! I'll be at The Grill."

At 11:30, while sitting in the Chill-Grill waiting on Tim to finish his business, Q notices two unknown niggas eyein' everything that is moving. The mirrors behind the bar serve their purpose well. Q can see them clearly. Just as Tim enters the door, the two men are easing past him, walking out. Q checks their attire from the mirrors without turning around. Instantly, he peeps that the tall, yellow, pretty-boy nigga is either packing, or he could rule the world with his dick. Tim eases on the barstool next to Q.

"Done deal, homie. Jazzy just scooped up that paper and rolled."

"Nigga, you should marry shorty 'cause she real," says Q. "She's already wifey nigga, no papers needed."

"Aight, keep slippin', some nigga will beat you to it."

"Listen at this, Shaka Zulu, mothafucka givin' marriage advice. A nigga that's taking care of ten wives," Tim says.

They laugh, then there's instant silence. Tim never turns his head in Q's direction. He follows his eyes in the mirrors in front of them. Someone is peeping through the doors of the lounge.

"Yo', you peep homie?"

"Yeah, I noticed it before you came in. You straight?" Q asks.

"Just like American Express nigga. You just sit tight and let me go handle this shit."

"Nah, nigga. It isn't you they are checkin'." Q shakes his head.

While standing and stretching, Q eases his gun from its holster and slides it in the front of his waistband.

Q walks straight out the front door onto the sidewalk. Tim is about three steps behind. He looks right and left before he spots the two men leaning on a Suburban talking to two more guys.

"Damn nigga, you paranoid as hell. Them niggas on some other type shit," says Tim.

Q's years of street knowledge tells him different. He knows stick up boys when he sees them, but maybe, just maybe, he is wrong this time.

"Maybe you right, let's get to the club. Where you parked?"

"Around the corner," Q points out.

"I'm over in the parking lot, so I'll meet you around The Block," Tim lets Q know.

With that, they split up. Q crosses directly in front of the 'burban. He notices Texas license plates on the front bumper. As soon as they lock eyes, he knows never to doubt his instincts again.

"What up nigga, do I know you?" Pretty-boy says in an arrogant way.

Q's blood is boiling, but he remains calm. He is out numbered and doesn't know how many are strapped.

"I don't know? Do you know me?" Q inquires.

Pretty-Boy makes a move to his left toward the backdoors on the truck, just as Q is about to pull for his gat. He hears guns being clicked. It is coming from behind him.

"Problem here niggas? Is there a mothafuckin' problem niggas?" It is Tim and some other cat with what looks to be a Mack-10. Instantly, people begin scattering for cover, leaving only the seven men. Q is thinking "never let your anger dictate your actions." He is about to diffuse the situation when Pretty-Boy breaks for his back door. Boom-Boom... Blak-Blak-Blak-Blak... Boom. The men take off running, except Pretty-Boy, who has taken two hollow points to the abdomen and one to the lower rib cage, but he is still living. That's until the unknown cat with Tim jumps up and moves with the speed of a Bengal tiger and plants two more shots to his head. Sirens can already be heard in the background as the three make their escape.

"Let's get the hell out of here. I'll meet y'all at the club," yells Q as he begins to run.

<hr>

Club Mercedes is wall to wall. Sizing up the crowd, Q already knows the fire chief's pockets are fat. As soon as he enters the double doors, he stands still until his eyes adjust to the dim lights. He eases over to the bar to get his usual drink, a plain coke.

"What's up Quentel?" says the lady behind the bar. "What can I get you to drink? It's on me".

"Oh yeah? Well if that's the case, I'll have you with two cubes of ice."

Her name is Alien, and she is fine, but she is no fool. She knows Q has a woman for every day of the week. And she is not trying to become a part of his stable.

Alien responds, "I better take a rain check tonight, sexy. Besides, Tee and Van are here, so the tension will be thick enough."

Q loves Tee to death, but Van is his first true love. Their on-again off-again relationship is only because of his mishaps and fuck-ups. Her love for him is as pure as gold. Whenever he needs comfort or peace of mind, she is there with open arms. Van knows she is his heart. She doesn't have to flaunt it for other bitches to know either. She knows she is the one who had the longevity with Q.

The dance floor is jam packed. Everyone is facing the stage waiting for The Ying-Yang Twins to perform. Q sips his drink slowly as he relives the events that happened earlier that night.

Who were those fools? he thought. *What were they doing on his set? And why did they pick him to fuck with?*

The DJ announces that the show will begin in fifteen minutes. Everyone rushes to the bar to get their drinks before show time. Q eases from his stool and begins making his way through the crowd. Before he can blend in good, someone reaches out and grabs his hand.

It's Van, all 4'11" of her. Van is a chocolate bombshell. She is darker than the darkest night, but her skin is flawless. What she lacks in height, she makes up in heart.

On more than one occasion, Q's female friends found out shorty is not to be fucked with. One afternoon, Omar paged Q and told him Tee was waiting on Van with some friends of hers in the neighborhood. Q almost blew his Mustang up trying to get home. When he finally got there, it was over, and he thought Tee had hurt Van. But as soon as he stepped out of his car, Omar filled him in on what happened.

"Man, you're not going to believe this shit. Van got out on Tee!" Omar says.

"What? Get the fuck outta here nigga!"

"I'm serious. I mean, I broke them up and all, but she got the best of her."

Q couldn't believe his ears. Tee is pretty nice with the hands to be a woman. She shadow boxes him all the time at home. Q stopped by Van and her mother's house to check up on her. He rang the doorbell once before her mother answered. She was visibly upset at what had gone down. Van is her only child, and they were close.

"How you doing Mrs. Ellerbe? I want to apologize for what happened." She gave a half hearted smile and pointed toward Van's bedroom. Q could hear Van's shower running as he entered her room.

"Yo' shorty, come up outta there," Q hollered.

"Just a minute Baby." Baby, Q thought? She just finished fighting one of my girls and she's still calling me Baby. Now he was really confused. Ten minutes later, Van shook a half asleep Q awake.

"Damn, what took you so long?" Van asked.

"It was only ten minutes Q and you just fell asleep," she said while sitting on the edge of her bed beside him with only a towel wrapped around her. She handed him a bottle of watermelon/raspberry body lotion, his favorite. She stood up in front of him and dropped her towel. Q reached out and stuck his index finger in and around her belly button. She began to moan from his touch.

"Baby, are you okay? Are you hurt anywhere?" Q said.

"Hurt? The only thing that hurts is Omar stopped it before I could finish that trick off," she said as she grabbed Q's hand and put it around her slim waist.

"I love you, more than life itself. Never once have I considered cheating on you. Baby, don't let this hustle game, these streets, and these dizzy bitches that don't really love you for you, ruin what we made plans to have ever since we carved our names in that tree," she said as she pointed out her bedroom window.

Q could see the sincerity in her eyes, and it crushed his heart. After all the dirt he had done, she stood strong, living up to her promise she had made to him as a teenager that she would always be by his side through thick and thin. Holding her warm body in his arms, he could feel the moisture from her tears on his shoulder.

"I love you too," was all he could muster up the strength to say, as they held one another for hours.

"Here, Baby," Van says, handing Q her spare condo key as she embraces him. He steps back and takes the key from her hand. She has on a tight fitting Prada mini dress which matches her dark skin. Van never has to wear make-up. Her beauty is natural. She is wearing a chain around her neck with the word ONE. Q had given it to her as a gift and a promise that they would always be just that... ONE.

"What up, ma?" Q yells over the music.

"You," she says.

"Nah. It's got to be you. And what I tell you about all that exposure," he says while eyeing her up and down.

"Boy, don't start trippin' over a dress you bought," she yells as she puts her hand on her hip.

"Aight now. I just don't want to have to get up in one of these nigga's ass tonight. I've already had some problems on The Block, and I'm not up for more drama."

Van senses his uneasiness and suggests they leave.

"We can get up out of here if you want, baby."

"I can't right now because I haven't seen Tim yet, and he is supposed to meet me here. Besides, your cousins Vet and Netra are looking pretty impatient over there waitin' on you."

"Well, that's tough shit. And anyway, I'm sleeping with you, not them," she says with a smirk on her face.

"Na, enjoy yourself. I'll see you later tonight," Q tells her.

With that said, she heads toward her table. Q watches her until she sits down with her cousins before he starts making his way towards the front of the stage where Tee and Elbony are sitting.

Damn this shit's packed he thinks, as he squeezes through the crowd. When he finally reaches Tee's table, he is surprised to see Omar there with Kiki. Kiki hardly ever comes to the club.

"What up everybody?" Q says as he pulls out his chair beside Tee. Instantly, he notices her attitude.

"It's almost 1:00, Q. What took you so long?" says Tee.

He takes a deep breath and is about to answer when the lights dim and the DJ begins introducing The Ying Yang Twins. The crowd goes wild when Lil John enters first saying, "YEA." They rock all of their latest joints including "Shake It Like a Salt Shaker" and the strippers go crazy. Given the signal, Omar and Q step away from the table and make their way to the office in the back. Once inside, Big Kev waves them in another door that reads PRIVATE.

"Damn nigga, how many strippers you got out on that mothafucka tonight?" Q says to Big Kev.

"Stopped counting at twenty nigga, why?"

"Cause them bitches probably makin' more money than all of us together, that's why."

Q begins dialing Tim's cell number. The phone inside the desk drawer starts to ring. Big Kev pulls the phone from the drawer and shows it to Q. He shuts his flip phone and grabs Tim's.

"So that nigga did make it here, huh?"

"Yeah, he's at the bar with some new cat. He told me what went down on The Block. Shit's going to be hotter than a mothafucka for a few days."

"Yeah, I'm hip nigga. Them four bama's had a death wish or something."

"Well, they always say be careful what you wish for."

"That nigga at the bar with Tim, he is as thorough as they come. He didn't even blink before letting that Mac-10 go!"

'Code-Red Code-Red' is all you can hear blasting on Kev's radio. All three jump up and head out the door. The commotion is coming from down at the booth where Shea and Tab are collecting money. Two niggas are standing outside of a Big Boy Benz complaining about being checked for weapons. Big Ant is explaining the situation to them as calmly as he can, but they aren't trying to hear that shit. Cars are honking their horns behind them, trying not to miss the rest of the show.

Q stops at the booth to check up on the situation.

"What's the problem?" he asks.

"Just two niggas actin' up, thinkin' they VIP or somethin'," says Tab.

"Yeah."

"Yeah. They both packin' but don't want to leave their shit."

Q looks the Benz over. Da Da is on the license plate. He only knows of one person by that name. He is a money-getting' nigga from outta Wadesboro, N.C. While Big Kev and Ant are flagging other cars around the stopped car, Tim and the new cat from The Block slowly walk up on the situation.

"Yo,' Q. What tha fuck is this 'Code Red' shit? You got problems down this bitch or what?" Tim says.

"Who you nigga?" the guy on the passenger side says to Tim.

"I'm the coroner nigga."

"What up Da Da?" a voice can be heard over the split second of silence.

"What's the problem?" Q says, creeping up almost motionlessly, sliding his gun from its holster under his left arm. He conceals it from the cars waiting behind him as best as he can, not wanting to cause a panic toward the crowd.

"What up Q?" Da Da says in a surprised tone.

"What up homie? What's the problem?"

"Ain't no problem, man. I just don't like parting with my girlfriend," he says, patting his waistband.

"Rules of the game playa, nothin' personal. Now, you can either put your 'girlfriend' in the booth, or you can turn this shit around and go party elsewhere."

"Oh, it's like that, huh?" Da Da asks.

"Yeah, it's like that homie. And for future reference, you need to put a bridle and bit in your horse's mouth," he says pointing to the guy on the passenger side. "If he ever tries to make some noise on this side of town again, I will personally dig up in that ass."

Da Da and his partner are heated, but they know better than to try something stupid. It will surely prove fatal. Everyone nearby can hear the confrontation, and that only makes Da Da's want for revenge more personal. He glares hard at Q before sliding in his Benz and yanking a three point turn leaving. Tim walks up and puts his hand on Q to motion him back to the club.

"Oh yea, this is my man June," Tim says.

Q gives June some dap before getting into a conversation. "Man, you're a hard nigga to catch up wit."

"I just don't meet many people homie," Q responds.

"He wants to join The Crew," Tim says.

"Yeah playa, whatever I gotta do to be in, I'm game."

Q knows he has a hair trigger. He can tell that from The Block. *A man like that is always good to have on your team,* he thinks. But it's something else about him Q really likes. Maybe it's the fact that he sees himself in June. A few years back, he would have killed first and asked questions later. However, time and experience has made him cautious.

"We'll meet tomorrow at Grady's on the set and discuss business, aight?" Q asks.

"Aight. Well let's get back up in this club wit these hoes," June says.

"Yeah, that nigga Da Da, got me all fucked up. I'm a see that nigga again, and it's going to be on," says Tim.

Chapter Two

Getting Paid

The Crew's stash house is located three houses down from the mayor's home. They know more about the mayor's wife than he does. The Crew have a couple of officers on the payroll. Some strictly for giving information on raids, and others are hauling kilos by night. Both are supposed to be serving and protecting the community during the day.

"Everything's ready," Corey yells from his car window. "The Brew is in place."

With that, Q heads to their cook house. He stops by the Purina dog food place and picks up a hundred and fifty pounds of food for his pitbulls. He knows he will have to cut back soon, but he doesn't know where to start. He knows every dog's match weight and keeps them semi-conditioned in case some of the local hustlers bring one of 'their curs by to get stopped'. Turning onto the dirt road, Q can see two of his boys holding their position on lookout. One can never be too careful in this game. With all the stick-up boys trying to come up, along with the Po-Po raiding people's shit, The Crew doesn't take any chances. Pulling behind the house, he can't hear all his dogs greeting him. He has a two time winner named Skull who always makes his presence known by running at full speed, yanking himself off his feet. Any other breed of dog would have broken their neck. This particular dog has already been over the two hour mark in the pit. At twenty minutes into the fight, Skull suffered a broken leg. He went the other hour and fifty-two minutes on three legs and a truck load of heart. He is dead game, but would give his life for Q in or out of the pit.

"Yo' Q, you ready to do this homie?" It's Corey standing on the back patio. "Everybody's in place."

"Aight, let's do it." He tosses his cell phone and pager in his front seat and walks inside the house. Everything is in order as usual. "I brought fifteen joints from the mayor's house, homie (the downtown stash house)."

"Oh, yeah. Did you kiss his wife for me?" Q says with a smirk on his face.

"Nah, nigga, but I did get some brain from her ass!"

Putting on his latex gloves and mask, Q begins the long process of cooking fifteen kilos. The Crew has really blown up since his main connect, Dreadlock AKA Baby Rasta man, taught him how to whip his coke, turning fifteen into thirty. After about six hours, Q finally finishes his last two. Before he is half way through, ten are already gone.

"You nigga's gonna have to learn how to cook this shit man. I'm stepping down in about seven, eight months tops. I won't be coming out of retirement to cook this shit for you niggas."

None of The Crew wants to accept the fact that Q is serious, but they know he is. He has mentioned it a lot lately. They also know he isn't the type of nigga to say shit just to be saying it.

"Aight, you nigga's can hit me later," Q says, grabbing the duffel bag containing damn near two hundred thousand dollars.

"Tim, you and Corey divide the shit that's left. I'm out. Peace," Q says.

Once inside his car, Q checks his two-way. He has thirty-four messages. His baby momma texted him a couple of times from her cell. Q considers himself and his daughter lucky to have such a good baby momma. Keonne is six years old. She always calls on Thursday to remind him the weekend starts the next day. On Friday, she stands at the door waiting to spend the weekend with her daddy. Q loves his daughter to death and wouldn't trade her for anything in the world. But like any man, he wants a son desperately. He has tried to have a child with Van, but she is unable to maintain a full pregnancy. She has suffered some damage to her uterus as a child and has never been able to overcome it.

Tee also calls and wants Q to stop by and see her new salon.

After driving to his hideaway spot on the outskirts of town, he pulls up inside his four car garage. After the automatic door closes, he jumps out and enters the house. His rot, Bear, stands at the door waiting. Bear growls when he walks in. "What's your problem boy? I been gone too long, huh? Aight, let's get something to eat." Bear's automatic feeder is still half full, so Q knows Van had to have been by earlier. She is the only person who knows anything about this house, and two more properties Q had purchased. He bought Bear for her as a gift.

Entering the kitchen on the way to his safe, he notices one single white rose with an envelope:

My Dearest Q,

By the time you read this letter, I'll be back at our place rubbing on your favorite body lotion. My heart almost leaped out of my chest when you told me you were getting out of the game. So many nights I prayed this day would come. Soon, I won't have to worry about you being safe... I'll have you in the safety of my arms. You are my life, my love, my everything.

Your soul-mate, Van

Closing the letter Q knows this is his true love. The only question in his mind is how he would be able to explain all this to Tee when the time came.

THE TRUCK FINALLY ARRIVES AT THE BUILDING THAT WILL SOON BE called "Honey's."

"It's about time they get here," says Tee.

"Yeah, we've been here almost two hours," El responds.

The truck is bringing three new dryers for the salon. One of the movers says, "Sorry for the delay ma'am. Our truck broke down, so we had to load everything onto another truck. Where would you like your merchandise?"

The Grand Opening is next Thursday. Tee knows her dream is about to become a reality. She has put in a lot of hours in the living room doing hair. She has everything she has ever asked for. Well, almost everything. She loves her man to death, but is growing tired and weary from competing for his heart.

"Damn Tee, we finally gonna do it," says El.

"Yeah, sometimes I can't believe we're opening our own shop."

"Well gurl, please believe it. It's ours. But I've gotta go pick up my mother, so call me at home tonight."

"Aight. I'm gonna call Q and see if he's coming or not."

"Okay, but don't stay here too long by yourself."

"Okay Mama," Tee says, rolling her eyes and waving her arms in the air. She grabs her cell phone and gives Q a call.

Q answers his phone, "Yes."

"Hey Baby, I've been calling you," she says.

"Sorry ma, I got a little tied up, but I'm on my way now. You want me to stop and get you something?"

"Well, I'm finished here for tonight, so I am thinking we could go out for Chinese food."

"Sounds good to me. I'm game if I can have you for dessert!"

"Okay, but what about my dessert mister?"

"You'll think of something before I get there won't you?"

"I have something already in mind, hmm... hmm... hmm..."

"Stop teasing me Tee before I blow this mothafucka up trying to get there."

"Aight baby, but please hurry. I'm starving... Not for food either!" With that she hangs up while Q is stripping gears and cussing. Laughing, Tee leans back in her office recliner as her mind drifts back to the day she met Q.

It was at a local high school football game. He was with his boys. But something about him demanded attention. Not just from the women either. He had a body that looked like he was carved with a sledge hammer and chisel. He was so fine. Although she had never seen God, she felt like this was what he would look like. Q was definitely the total package.

"Elbony, Elbony," Tee said as she grabbed her girlfriend's arm, almost pulling her down.

"Damn girl, what is it? You trying to break my arm or something?"

"Who is that?" Tee said, cutting her eyes and shaking her head in his direction.

"Oh, him? That's only Q," Elbony said as she turned around to order some popcorn.

"Only Q, huh? So you know him El? Do you know him well enough to introduce us?"

"Well, yes and no."

"What da hell does that mean?"

"Him and my brother Chez are cool. He comes over from time to time. Chez introduced him to The Game, even though he's a year older than him."

"Yo' Q, ain't that Chez's sister El over there?" said Umar.

"Yeah, that's her. Let me go holla at her, and check up on my nigga."

"Oh my God El, he's coming over here girl. I can't breathe," said Tee.

Q spoke to El. "What up lil' sis? What's good wit you?"

"Hi Q," she said, giving him a hug. "It's been a while."

"Yeah, I know. Please forgive me for staying away so long. And what's your name cutie-pie?" he said, reaching for Tee's hand.

"It's Tashonda, but you can just call me Tee."

"Well it's nice to meet you Tee." He turned to El.

"Well lil sis', it is good seeing you. And tell Chez to give me a call."

"Aight big brother," she said before hugging him again.

Q turned to Tee. "Come here ma," he said before hugging her too. Holding her in his arms he whispered, "Please don't let this be the last time I hold you." Then he planted a soft kiss on her earlobe. "Call me anytime," he said, then returned to his crew.

From that night on, they talked on the phone for hours at a time. They hung out together at least four days out of the week. He even told her *about his on again off again relationship with Van. She listened to all his problems and never once did he make any sexual passes at her. She was beginning to wonder what was taking him so long.*

One Friday night, Q invited Tee over to his place. Keonne and her mother were going to Carowinds for the weekend, so he was free. When she arrived, she was greeted at the door by Q, who was leaning over like his back was killing him. "What's up Tee?"

"What happened to you Q?"

"I don't know ma. I think I pulled a muscle at the gym today."

There goes my great night she thought. "You don't need to be walking around like that. Did you get it checked?"

"Nah. But if it's not better by tomorrow, I'm going to the doctor."

"Well at least take a hot shower and bath before you lie down on it. I'll get the water ready."

"Thanks Boo."

Q stood in the shower with the water as hot as he could stand it.

"Q, I put your towels out here with your robe," she yelled over the running water.

Pulling back the shower curtain, he reached out and waved her back to him. "Come here Boo."

She was so caught off guard that he pulled her right into the shower with her tank top and shorts on. Q planted kisses on her forehead while removing her clothes piece by piece. Once undressed, he slowly kissed her neck and made his way down to her firm breast. She moaned from his touch.

"But baby, what about your back?"

"Baby, I've got a four-hundred pound bench press. Raising these two thighs is just what the doctor ordered."

Lifting her from the shower, he walked to his adjoining bedroom and laid her wet body on his bed. Exhausted from the work he had just put in, he closed his eyes and went to sleep. Q was awakened by his own moans. Tee had recuperated and was back for revenge.

The phone startles Tee from her day dreaming.

"Hello, Honey's Beauty Salon. Yes, we're accepting appointments. The Grand Opening is next week, and we will be open for business at 9: 00 a.m. Friday. Can I make your appointment for 12:00 p.m. ma'am?

That will be fine. Thank you, and I look forward to seeing you then." Hanging the phone up, Tee sits back and counts her blessings. Then gives thanks to God. She has almost a full schedule. She picks up the phone and calls her girl Elbony.

"Hello."

"Hey girl, I see you made it home okay," she says.

"Yeah, girl. I'm on the phone wit a nigga I met at the mall name Da Da. He gettin' money too gurl."

"Aight El, but be careful and don't go nowhere without me knowing. You know how them money getting' niggas are."

Tee hears a knock at her door.

"Well gurl, I've gotta go. Q just walked in. Call me tomorrow. Bye." She turns to Q. "My, didn't we get here quick."

"Very funny Tee, very funny. Anyway, I took the long way here," he says, trying not to laugh.

"So, you've been at the gym huh?" El says gazing at the gym bag and Under Armor tank top.

"Yeah, I stopped by for about an hour or so."

"Did you bring something to wear out to eat?"

"I didn't know we were going to dinner ma. I thought you said Chinese food."

"I did Boo, but..."

"But what? I've left the gym a thousand times dressed like this, stopped and gotten you Chinese. And they damn sho' ain't got no drive thru."

"Okay nigga, but if I catch one eye on your ass too long, then I guess we won't be eating Chinese food there anymore. Now come give mama a kiss."

"But I'm sweaty!"

"Nigga, bring yo' ass here. You don't say that when you got my ass looking at our bedpost at home!"

Chapter Three

Money, Power, Respect

Honey's has become one of the most exclusive salons in town. If you don't make your appointment a week prior, you are subject to be ass out for at least two weeks.

It's Friday afternoon when the drama jumps off. All three chairs are full with the waiting area wall to wall packed. Tee has hired another girl named Terri. Terri is the type of girl who is beautiful and built, and she knows it. She makes sure everyone else knows it too. As far as men are concerned, if you aren't thugged out and ridin' on those big things, you don't even need to waste yo' time.

"Look up Tee. He's pulling up on time for a change. You must have given him a little bit last night," says El.

"No, sweetheart. I gave him a lot last night," Tee says, giving El the finger.

Walking inside, Q says to everyone. "I brought ya'll some lunch."

"Thanks Baby, it would have been hours before one of us could go get something."

His two-way beeps. Checking it, he sees that it is his connect, Baby Rasta man's code. "Babe, I'll be in the office. I have to make a call."

Terri is watching the whole scene from in the cut. *Damn that nigga smooth* she thinks. My ex-boyfriend Tex is hating when he says Q is a regular nigga. Pulling off this job might be more difficult than a bitch thought.

"Is there something wrong Terri? You look like you've seen a ghost," says Tee.

"Oh, oh no, just daydreaming, that's all."

"Well, if you keep daydreaming and forget about that perm in front of you, Miss Tracy gonna get up, and she's gonna be Miss Isaac Hayes!"

Everyone erupts in laughter, except Tee.

Tee figures making a joke is the best way to deal with Terri. But inside, she's really thinking, *This bitch must think I'm stupid, daydreaming my ass. I don't mind a bitch looking but don't undress my man right in front of me, then expect me not to notice.* She makes a mental note to watch this trick real close.

"Somebody has company," Terri yells as she sees a big body Benz pulling up out front. El sees Da Da out the window and waves for him to come inside.

"Yo' Tex, I'll be right back homie," says Da Da.

"Nah, nigga. All them bad bitches I see up in there. I'm going in wit' yo' ass."

After entering the salon, El makes all the formal introductions.

Terri shakes Tex's hand like she doesn't even know him.

Q is still on the phone in the back with Rasta man.

"What's up Rasta?"

"Yea mun, what took you so long mun? You dissing me mun?"

"Come on Rasta, you know better than that. Besides, I called as soon as you hit me."

"Aight mun. How's business?"

"Good Ras, good."

"Have you married tha young lady you brought down to the island mun?"

Q had taken Van to Jamaica to visit Rasta Man's family. Q never did forget how they fell in love with her. "Marry her mun, marry her," is all they kept saying.

"Nah, Ras. I haven't married her yet, but soon."

"Okay mun, but don't make it too late you know."

"Aight, Ras. I'll see you on Saturday."

Q hangs up the phone and walks back into the work area.

"Tee, I'm gone ma but call me before you're ready to lock up." He can hear a lot of commotion coming from the lobby area.

"Damn Tee, what tha hell is that?"

"Just the customers and two guys here to see El."

"Terri, can you watch my client for a second? I'm going outside," El says.

Q looks in the lobby area and sees the two men "Well, I be damned. If it ain't Da Da and Seabiscuit, his horse," he says to Tee.

"You know them, Q?"

"Yeah. They the ones who don't want to give up their heat at the club."

"Did they cause any trouble?"

"They got a little upset, but it couldn't have been that bad cause they still livin'," he says with a wink.

"Do you want them to leave?" Tee asks.

"Nah, ma. I ain't trippin'. Besides, I have a couple of runs to make."

Walking through the lobby, Da Da and Tex spot Q walking toward them. "What up, Q?"

"What up, Da?"

"Nothin' much, just swingin' through to holla at Elbony."

Q didn't even look Tex's way.

"Aight Da Da, hold it down."

With that he turns and walks straight out the salon, not looking back.

Chapter Four

Getting Out the Game

Business is booming. All of the crew is getting plenty of money.

"You niggas need to invest some of that paper. I'm not talkin' about no cars and shit like that."

It is hard for Q to explain the car situation to The Crew because when he first started out, that's all his boys remembered about him.

"Look fellas, I'm not sayin' don't treat yo' self. All I'm sayin' is put something up for a rainy day."

He taught Tim how to cook, so the only time Q is at the cook house is when he checks up on his dogs. He has already purchased some more land to move his kennel to. Slowly, he is making due his promise to Van. He doesn't want to leave Tee with nothing, so he makes sure she is straight with her business. Even The Crew don't realize he is fading out of the picture.

One day while driving to the mall in Charlotte, Van pulls her red Honda Civic into an Auto Bell carwash to have it detailed.

"It's about time you clean this damn car," says Q.

"Just get out and stop complaining. You were supposed to do it two weeks ago. And guess who's driving the rest of the way for that comment?"

"Come on ma. We're only in Wadesboro. We still have over an hour. You know my back catches cramps in this matchbox!"

The carwash has a McDonald's attached to it, so they decide to grab something to eat and enjoy the sunny day. "You order us something to eat while I find us a table outside," says Van.

While sitting down, talking, and eating their food, Tex, Da Da, and two other guys pull into the car wash on their bikes.

"Yo, Da Da, do you see what I see?" says Tex. "Now it's funny how a nigga can get on another set and change his whole disposition."

"Yeah, I see that nigga. He got a lot of fame on the other side of the bridge, but he's on our set now."

"Look at that nigga. Punk bitch, looking scared to death," Tex cocks up.

Q turns to Van. "Van, remember what we worked on at home with the stick-up situation?"

"Baby, wha..."

"Shhh, listen to me Boo. I want you to get up and go get the car. Pay 'em, get in it, and drive across the street to that convenience store."

"But Ba..."

"Do it now!" Q demands with harshness in his voice.

"Okay Baby, I'm going," she says, raising up and slowly opening her purse to show him her .380.

"Nah, ma, hold that. I got my shit on me," he says patting his left arm pit. "Now go on."

Once Q is able to see Van across the street, he breathes a sigh of relief. A few more cats come up and begin a conversation with Da Da and his boys.

"Come on niggas, let's get this over wit'," Q says to himself.

"Man, let's do this nigga," Tex says to Da Da. "I'm sending that nigga back to Rockingham in a bag."

"Be careful Tex. You know that nigga packin'."

"So fucking what? We all packin' nigga. Come on," Tex confidently says.

Q relaxes in his chair and waits until they are about ten feet from his table. He lets one hand swing down, exposing his gat. All four stop dead in their tracks.

"You nigga's got anybody you want me to call?"

"Call for what nigga?" asks Tex.

"So, I can let them know what your last words were."

"Slim, you might get one of us, but yo' ass is dead... You outnumbered nigga," says Da Da.

"Are you sure Da Da?" Q asks with a smirk on his face.

"Hell yeah, I'm sure nigga. I can count."

"Aight nigga, wit' yo' good counting' ass. Did you count that nigga standin' in the phone booth?"

They all look back in time to see June slide his coat back, giving them a look at his Mac-10 with the extended clip.

"What about them three cats over there washing the Caddy?" Tim, Omar, and Big Kev all have street-sweepers.

At that point, they know they walked into a death trap. "Let me explain something to you Da Da. You and ya' man. What we do at The Club is nothing personal. We have to protect the crowd. So what happens here today is on me. The next time it will be on you. There's no turf anywhere in N.C. I can't go and get respect nigga, cause I give it. The next time we cross paths homie, I'll make it my duty to bleed yo' bitch ass. You and ya' boy."

With that said, Q stands up, walks right between them and crosses the street to the store's parking lot. Getting in the passenger side, he notices Van drying tears from her face.

"It's aight ma. Everything is aight."

"But what about the next time, Baby? If something happens to you, I can't live. Don't you understand that Q? You're all I've got. Baby, listen to me. I want us to be together, just me and you. Fuck all those other bitches, please just come back home to me," Van begs.

"Aight Van, but I have a lot of loose ends to tie up. Now what was you gonna do with that?" Q says pointing at the .380 in her lap.

"I was comin' across that damn street and get my soulmate. We have a future planned together boy, and I'm lookin' forward to livin' it!"

"I love you, ma."

"I love you more. Now let's go shopping."

The rest of the day was uneventful. Q let Van shop till she dropped.

While Van is in Victoria's Secret, he doubles back to the jewelry store they were at earlier.

"I see you came back huh?" says the sales lady.

She is white, but her skin is dark for a white girl. It's evident she spends a lot of time at the beach or on her patio.

"Yes ma'am, I..."

"Call me Kris," she says, reaching out to touch his hand.

"Aight Kris, I would like to peep at that ring we looked at earlier?"

"Sure."

Turning on her heels, she went to get the ring Van had fallen in love with. It is a three and a half carat diamond in a platinum setting. When she returns, he already has his Platinum Card out.

"You can go ahead and put a ribbon and bow on that one, Kris."

After checking his credit, she has his gift wrapped. *This white girl is smoking Q* thought. *Damn, she been doing some squats too. Ain't no white girl's ass that fat without putting in some type of work in the gym.*

"Can I get you anything else, Mister?"

"Well, since I get to call you Kris, just call me Q."

"Well, can I get you anything else, Q?"

"As a matter of fact, Kris, I'll take you wrapped in that big bow over there," he says in a joking manner.

"I get off at 8:oo."

"Huh?" Q says, caught off guard.

"I said that I get off at 8:oo, but I see you're busy tonight," she says, patting the ring he just bought. "Maybe next time though. Here's my cell phone and home number. I live alone so call anytime."

"Okay. I'll give you a call tomorrow."

"Damn this day might turn out good after all," Q says to himself. Making his way back to the Victoria's Secret store where Van is, Q puts the box inside his jacket pocket. He will surprise her with it over dinner.

"Baby, how are you planning on carrying all this shit to the car? You need to hire your own personal caddy."

"I already got one," she laughs. "With a strong back. Now let's go love, we have two more stops to make."

Finally after leaving the GNC Store, which is the only thing Q came for, they go to TGIF's on Harris Blvd. Over dessert, Q sits Van down and discusses future plans.

"Boo, look. I've been slowly breaking my bond from The Game. Not my boys, but The Game. My heart has been left in those streets ma." Tears began to roll down Van's face. "Babe, please don't start that. You know how I am about you when you start cryin'."

"Don't worry babe, these are tears of joy. Now, finish what you started."

"What I'm saying is, I've made so many different situations out there in those streets that sometimes I feel like I'm obligated to those too. Now it's hard to get away from a lot of those things without drama."

"Meaning Tee, huh?" she questions.

"Not only Tee, I mean the streets in general. Just my name and reputation brings drama."

"But it has to start somewhere."

"It is Boo, it's starting today." He glimpses down, pulling the gift wrapped box out his coat pocket.

"What's this Q?" Van asks with a shocked look on her face.

"Open it ma." Q nods his head in her direction, giving her permission to open the box.

Van is speechless. Tears stream down her face uncontrollably.

"Babe, stop cryin'."

"I can't help it Q, it's beautiful."

"Does that mean that you'll be my wife?"

"I'm already yo' wife, boy. We're just making it official. All that other stuff is only temporary."

"Look Van, I'm gonna need a little time to break all this to Tee, but I will take care of it."

"I've had trust in you from day one Q, and I trust you now. Take as much time as you need. You're my love, my life, my everything."

Chapter Five

Shut 'Em Down, Open Up Shop

It is now two months later, and Q has officially retired from The Game. He moved Van into a private suburban home on the outskirts of town. Even The Crew know nothing about their hideaway in the gated community. Tee went ballistic when Q moved out of their Town Park apartment.

"What do you mean you're leaving Q? What have I done besides love you? Huh? This is how you do me?"

"It's not you Tee, it's me. I've got my own reasons for going."

"Yeah, I'll bet you do. Tell that bitch it ain't over. You are my man, Q. I'm not giving you up without a fight."

Q had to admit she has been a great woman to him and he did have love for her. But Van is the woman he wants to spend his life with. Is there another way to do this? If only he can make both of them happy.

"Well, I better be going. If you ever need anything, you know I will be here for you, don't you Tee?"

"I need your love, Boo. That's all I'm missing." With that, she plants a soft kiss on Q's lips before whispering the words "I Love You." Unable to look her in the eyes, he turns and walks out of the office then out of the salon.

Tim, Omar, and June have turned up the heat on The Block. They even opened up another spot inside a trailer park.

"Yo' what up fellas?" Q says, pulling up on his suke.

"What's up my nigga? I see you still ridin' that slow shit," says Tim.

"Yeah, nigga, you tryin' to see me?" he says, pointing at his nitrous bottle. "I still don't have to turn it on to beat yo' ass."

Q spends most of his weekends at the local track racing his three bikes. Between that and his dogs, he barely has time for anything else.

"Come on nigga, let me show you our new spot," says Umar.

They ride out to their new spot, which is booming. "So how do you like our set-up?"

Looking over the spot, Q sees a bunch of flaws. Maybe it's just his street knowledge that brings them out. Nevertheless, they are there.

"Too many flaws homie. Check your entry way. Too much traffic coming in the same way. And where are your lookouts? They should be coming from the other end of the park. This should be your only exit. That way, people that live here can get in and out without problems. So, first thing you need to do is make one trailer your base. Get some walkie-talkies and bikes for your runners. Hire two lookouts. Keep everybody living here happy," Q says as he recognizes the flaws that could be costly down the line.

"Damn nigga, you done got the game and gone wit' it," says Umar.

"Ah, homie, I used to run tha game," Q says proudly.

Q knows the game isn't all the way out of him. At home, he has the habit of listening to the police scanner. He knows all the local narcotics agent's codes.

"Well, you niggas do it the way you been doing it. Hell, I'm out the game," he says thankful. "Speaking of being out, I've got to get out of here and get my ass home, you know a nigga on lockdown now," he states with a slight chuckle. He gives all the guys some dap and hops on his bike.

Nearly an hour later, Q arrives home. He can smell the fried chicken cooking through the door. He headed straight for the kitchen.

"Babe, you got the house smelling good," he says as he spots Van standing by the stove.

"Yea, I made your favorite... chicken, macaroni and cheese, with some corn on the cob." Van says as she walks over to receive a warm embrace.

"That's what's up! But damn, you didn't have to get dressed up to serve it to me," Q says as he releases her, and eyes her up and down.

"You stupid. I told you earlier, I'm gonna ride out to tha club wit' my cousins, you don't remember?"

"O yea, my fault. Tell my boys I say what's up. I would go, but I have to pick up Keonne in the morning."

"I won't be too long then," Van says as she navigates around the kitchen.

"Good, but come 'ere, before you go. I want to show you something," Q requests. Van walks over and stands between his legs. She is so short, he could sit on the edge of the chair and damn near still have to look down at her. He raised her 'BEBE' tee shirt up exposing her laced bra. "Can I taste you before you go?" he asks seductively

"Why start something you can't finish?" she replies awaiting his decision.

"You started it by looking so good." They laugh together.

He pulls her bra up, releasing her breast. Sucking them slowly, he moans from their taste.

"What time will your cousins get here?" he asks, never letting go of either breast.

"You've got twenty minutes tops, but please don't stop."

"Damn, that is good baby. You can go now. I know ain't no nigga followin' after that shit."

"You're so crazy," Van replies. "I'll see you when I get back."

"Aight. I think I'm going to watch some TV."

Q relaxes back into his oversize leather sofa. Beep... Beep ... Beep. Q reads the text on his phone. It's Kris. Q has seen Kris several times since meeting her in the jewelry store. His first sexual encounter with her was crazy. He thought she was gonna pass out when he pulled his clothes off. She had never been with a black man before, and it showed. It took a nigga damn near two whole hours to get it in. Now, she has done something her own parents would disown her for. She has fallen in love with a black man.

"What's up Kris?"

"Hi there, stranger."

"Stranger? It's only been two weeks."

"Yeah, but it seems more like a year."

"Well, what's on your mind?" he says, already knowing.

"Well, I know it's tha weekend, and you have to spend time with tha kids, so I'm hoping we could get together after work on Monday."

"That sounds good. I'll drive up Monday, early, before you get off."

"Good. Make sure you come by tha job and get the house key."

"Aight, bet. I'll see you then." Q hangs up.

The scanner has a 911 caller reporting a shooting. It has happened on The Block.

Damn, what the fuck's going on? Q thinks. He pages Umar then tries his cellphone. An unknown voice answers.

"Who tha fuck is this?" says Q.

"Don't worry nigga. Yo' boy dead. That's all you need to know." Beep, beep, beep is all Q hears as the unknown voice hangs up on him.

Jumping out of bed, Q throws on a sweatsuit and speeds to The Block. He dials Tim's cell on the way.

Tim answers, "Yo."

"Tim this is Q. Where tha hell you at nigga?"

"I'm on the way to the club nigga, why?"

"Forty-five nigga. Forty-five. Call the rest of The Crew." Parking a block over on Hood Street, Q checks his clip.

Cutting through backyards, he comes up behind the Chill-Grill. He can hear all the commotion coming from the front of the building. Slowly, he creeps around the corner. A couple of heads spot him and start calling his name.

"Sshhoosh!" He puts one finger to his lips. "What's going on around there?"

"Some guys stuck Umar up while he was serving Cam and Dirk. It looked like a set-up to me," says the crackhead that's twitching, undoubtedly high.

"What you mean a set-up?"

"Well, during the transaction, two guys walked up behind Umar. Then, Cam and Dirk walked off. They had hoods on, hiding their faces. After Umar gave them the 'yay,' the tall one opened fire on him. Blak!"

Walking-around the building, Q sees the crowd standing a few feet from the yellow tape. Everything looks to be moving in slow motion. Detectives are everywhere. Umar's corpse has been covered with a sheet, waiting for a family member to come identify him. Q's legs feel like logs in water as he steps under the yellow tape, walking towards Umar's body.

"Excuse me sir, this is a crime scene."

Q ignores the officer and kneels beside his man. Pulling the sheet back, Q feels nothing but emptiness, looking at his boy lying in his own blood.

"I promise you fam, whoever did this will die. I promise you homie. Don't worry homie, I got Kiki's back."

"Sir, sir, you're in the middle of a crime scene, tampering with evidence."

Q is about to go apeshit on the officer when Kiki shows up.

"No... No... Noooo," she cries. Two officers have to restrain her from coming under the yellow tape. Q runs and grabs her, pulling her away from the scene.

THE NEXT FEW DAYS ARE TOUGH. KIKI HASN'T EATEN A THING since Omar's death.

"Kiki, you have to eat something. Please don't do this to yourself," Tee tells her.

"I can't, Tee. I just can't," Kiki cries.

"You have to Kiki. Do it for Umar. He would go crazy knowing you lost so much weight."

Kiki isn't the only one in deep mourning. Q hasn't been out in three days. He has only been out of bed to go back and forth to the bathroom. Van pampers him, but also lets him have his space to mourn the death of his friend in private.

The following week, the memorial is held at the local high school gym. The place is packed. Before the funeral begins, Kiki springs a surprise on Tee.

"Why Tee, why did he have to die like that? What about the baby,

Tee? I'm three months pregnant!"

"What!!! You're what Kiki?"

"I'm pregnant Tee."

The only words Q says to Van are "Go ahead to the funeral ma, I love you." She nods her head and leaves for the memorial.

During the service, you can hear murmurs throughout the crowd about none of The Crew being there. After the eulogy, people start viewing the body. The whole building begins to tremble as about thirty-five to forty bikes pull up in front of the gymnasium. It's the whole Crew on their Suzukis, along with some of the local guys, paying their respects to their fallen comrade. Q is out front riding Umar's Double R. As other family members file out of the gym, The Crew all enter to say goodbye to their homie.

Weeks go by, and Q keeps to himself. He doesn't work-out, doesn't answer his cell phone or pager. None of The Crew, or Tee, can reach him. Van stays right by his side through it all. When he pushes her away, she gives him space. When he needs her shoulder, she is there. Finally, when she feels his grief becoming life threatening, she finally puts her foot down.

"Q, I love you Boo. The day I close my eyes for the last time, I will still be loving you. But I will not sit here and watch you die. Umar is gone, and God knows I miss and love him. But he would be ashamed if he saw you treating yourself like this. You're not the only one hurting, Q. What about the rest of The Crew? Have you even considered that they may be feeling like you? Do they have someone to mourn with, huh? Do they? What about Tee, Q? Yeah, I always knew that you were gonna make sure she is alright. That's because you have a pure heart. We're not enemies, Q. We're just in love with the same man. Check on the rest of your family. All of them. They need you, I need you. Kiki and Umar's son need you."

"Son?"

"Yeah, son. Kiki's pregnant with your Godson," she turns and goes to their bedroom.

The way Van speaks of Tee makes Q look at the woman he loves in a whole different light. They have been to blows over him. Always at one another's throat. But in one of the hardest times, she shows compassion for a woman that is deeply in love with her man. They have something most couples wish they had... bulletproof love. Leaving their couch, he enters the bedroom. Gently, he pulls the covers back not wanting to wake Van. He puts his arms around her and closes his eyes.

"Welcome back, baby," Van says, enjoying his touch.

"It's good to be back ma. I love you."

"I love you more."

With that said, they go to sleep.

Chapter Six

Murder is the Case

The Block has been like a ghost town since Umar's death. Everybody knows that The Crew's revenge will be brutal. The police department has put what they call a command post on one end of The Block. The local newspaper reports that it is put there because of all the violence and drug activity being conducted. But, both of The Crew's contacts downtown say it is put there to stop the retaliation of The Crew. June and Tim have gone shell. No one can believe that Cam and Dirk have gone off code. They know the rules. The Crew had shown them nothin' but love. Sometimes, they wouldn't even tax them on work. Now Cam and Dirk have broken the rules of The Game. Betrayal is the lowest anyone can go. When you betray somebody, you give up all rights and automatically place your whole family on death row.

"So Tim, how do we handle this?" June says, reaching for the door handle.

Tim grabs June's arm. "Wait homie, something ain't right." Q has schooled Tim well when it came to puttin' in work, and patience is key.

"You see that old pickup truck over there?"

"Yeah."

"Look at the tailpipe. It's steaming. The lights in the house are off homie. We've been here for almost three hours. Our target is sitting right in front of the window like he's tryin' to get noticed."

"Yeah T, you right. It's a set-up."

"No doubt homie."

"I wonder. Why would a mothafucka gettin' money sell himself short for a couple dollars?"

"Maybe it isn't about money, June. Money causes a lot of different things, playboy. Like jealousy, envy, malice, and hatred."

"Well, whichever one it is, it's going to cost him his life."

"Yeah, and everybody else in that house."

Slowly, they creep past the pickup truck, knowing they can be seen. June and Tim stare right at the two officers watching Cam's house. They want them to feel their presence.

When Tim and June tell Q what has happened, he is angry as hell. "You niggas did what? What the fuck are you two thinking about? Who do you think the cops gonna snatch up if this nigga comes up stinkin', huh?"

"Yeah, you're right homie. We're acting on feelings."

"You damn right you are acting nigga, but it isn't feelings. It's stupidity. There's no way we can act now. None of us. Umar is my man too. Whoever killed him, will pay with their life but at the right time. What we have to do now is let everything get back to normal. Then we will set all this shit straight."

***

THE BLOCK IS SLOWLY COMING BACK TO LIFE. THE POLICE department only park a car at the command post trying to make people think they are patrolling. Shit, the junkies have become so comfortable with it there, they sit and smoke crack on the hood.

Within weeks, Cam and Dirk grow tired of the surveillance on them. They are used to getting money. Both of them have ordered the department to take them off P.C. They are safe as long as they stay out of sight.

Kiki is showing now. Q and Van spend as much time as possible with her. She has become close friends with Van. At first, she feels awkward because she and Tee are also friends .

"Kiki, what did the doctor say?" Van asks on the way out of the hospital.

"He says I have a clean bill of health."

"Good, do you need anything else before we pick Q up?"

"Nah, we're already late, so we better be getting to the gym."

"What took you two so long? I've been waiting for over an hour."

"Sorry, Boo. It's my fault," says Van. "We made a few extra stops."

"You must have made a lot of extra stops," he says, kissing them both on the cheek. "Let's get something to eat, I'm starving."

They drive to a nearby food spot and settle in to eat. The way Q is treating Kiki, you would think she is carrying his child. She doesn't know Q has already made up in his mind that Umar's son will be treated as his own son.

Chapter Seven

For My Homie

"Yo, June! Isn't that that nigga Cam gettin' out of that car?" Tim says.

"Bingo, that's him."

Cam is walking into the Huddle House Restaurant like he is King Kong.

"Turn this mothafucka around homie," Tim yells.

They park at the Holiday Express Motel across the street. Tim and June walk to the restaurant's parking lot and wait for Cam to come out. At the counter, Cam turns and spots them out the window. He spreads his arms and makes a gesture like 'Not Here, Not Now'. June pulls back his coat and reveals his Mac. Tim yells for him not to shoot, but it's too late.

Cam dives to the floor as the Mac-10 starts spitting. June seems to be in a trance. He walks behind his Mac-10 like it is pulling him. Cam's cry could be heard for miles as he tries to make his getaway. Boom!!! Boom!!! Boom!!! Blak... Blak... Blak... Blak. Cam jumps out the window trying to make it to safety. Tim is waiting on him, the hammer cocked into position ready to fire.

"Who put you up to it nigga? Who paid you?" Tim questions him.

"Tim, man, I swear I didn't have anything to do with it."

"Who did then nigga?" he asks pointing his Mini-14 directly at Cam's chest.

"Please, don't shoot me man. It's this cat named Da Da and some nigga named Tex. The cat named Tex did all the shootin'. That's all I know homie."

"Today's yo' lucky day nigga. I'm a let you..." Before Tim could finish June cut in.

"Yeah nigga, it is yo' lucky day. Tell Umar I sent ya'." Blak... Blak... Blak.

After Cam's murder, the detectives snatch June up off The Block. He is the only one in The Crew who is known to carry a Mac-10. Luckily, he is smart enough to hide his heat. The police pick up twenty-seven Mac-10 shells at the crime scene and charge June with murder anyway. No gun means no concrete evidence.

"Hello, Honey's Hair Sal..." Tee is interrupted by the operator.

"You have a collect call from the Richmond County jail," the operator cuts in.

After accepting the call, Tee talks to June and then hangs up and texts Q with her emergency code. He hits her right back.

"Q, meet me at the salon ASAP."

"I'm on my way ma. You aight?"

"Yeah, I will explain everything when you get here."

Q sits in Tee's office and listens to her explain June's situation.

"Damn, Tee. I told them two niggas to stay on tha low-low. The Crew would be the first ones the cops investigate if anything happens to those cowards."

"He says they picked him up and charged him with murder. No weapon, no witnesses, nothing. The only thing he is told is that an informant says he carries a Mac-10."

"If he calls back, let him know my lawyer will be there in the morning," Q tells her.

"Okay. June says they didn't give him a bond."

"Maybe Mr. Williams can get him one. Anyway, if they don't got a weapon, they don't got no case." The office phone rings.

"Hello, Honey's Salon."

"What's up Tashonda, are you busy?"

"Oh, hi Dre. Can you call me later? Q's here." Click.

Well, damn, bye to you too. Dre thinks to himself.

"Who is that ma?" asks Q.

"That's one of Terri's friends I met at a hair show No Grease Salon in Charlotte is sponsoring."

"So, you're seeing someone?" he inquires, unable to hide the jealousy in his voice.

"No, Q. I'm not seeing anyone. He just kinda walked up and introduced himself to me."

"Oh, so now you two are just kickin' it huh?"

"We're only friends, Q. And before you start making those accusations that are in the back of your head... let me clear them up for you. You were the last person I thought about before I went to bed last night. You were the first person I thought about when I woke up this morning. So think before you speak."

Heated, he blurts out, "Well who the fu... Never mind ma. I'm a just go."

"Q," she yells as he walks toward the door. He stops and faces Tee.

"You're the last and only person who's fuckin' me, Boo. I loved you then and I love you now. I don't know how you're going to keep two wives serviced, but don't start lettin' your clutch slip on me nigga. The only reason you're insecure is because you haven't turned me on my stomach lately. Don't worry babe, this is yours." Stepping around him, she walks out of her office leaving him heated and defeated.

Later in the evening, June's bond is set at $500,000. June is out in four hours. He would have been out sooner, but the detectives hauled him back to the investigation room to question him about the murder that happened a few months earlier. He is ordered not to leave town while out on bail.

"Damn homie, what you tryin' to do, get a life sentence? You killed that nigga right uptown, two blocks from the courthouse."

"I would've killed that nigga in tha courthouse. They murdered Umar in cold blood. To me, he is just like the nigga who pulled the trigger... guilty, now sentenced to death."

Tim sits and tells the rest of The Crew what Cam had said before he was killed.

"We should have killed both them niggas," says Kev.

"Yeah, you're right, Big Kev. If we had, then Umar would still be here with us. Now, he'll never get to see his son."

Q thinks about Da Da and Tex. The Crew is right. He'd had two chances to have these nigga boys singing 'This is for my homies.' He has let them live. And it cost his man his life. A painful pill to swallow.

Q speaks up. "Aight, everybody listen up. The holidays are almost here. You all know Baby Rasta's gonna be closin' for business until after the New Year. He's already called me. I hope y'all got your ends straight. When I am buying, he gives me twenty-five or more over what I buy."

"We straight homie," says Tim.

"Good, enjoy your families over the holidays. On the 2nd, be ready to sit down and discuss dealin' wit' these two niggas."

"I hear you homie," says June, "and I have all the respect for you in the world. But if we catch them two bitches outta pocket, my Mac-10 and Tim's Mini One will make fo' sho Umar has some more company. This time it will be a package deal."

"I feel you homies, but we've got to be thinkin' on this shit."

"Yeah you're right Q, but it's hard waking up every mornin' knowing I'll never see Umar again. I feel like I'm lettin' him down, allowing these cowards to walk the streets. What about his soon to be son Q? Those two niggas go home every night to their kids homie."

As bad as Q hates to admit it, The Crew is right. If they don't smash these two niggas soon, others will try and play their hand. It will definitely be a blood-bath.

Q gives the word. "Aight Tim, if you catch Da Da or Tex outta pocket, put them hot boyz on they ass."

"Don't worry homie, closed casket. Case closed."

Chapter Eight

Betrayal

"**D**amn Da, what time did you tell this nigga to meet you?"

"Just chill, Tex. That nigga will be here. He ain't been able to get no money cause them P.G. niggas been on the look-out. I told you before nigga, be 'bout yo' business when it comes to any of them cats. All them niggas love that gun play. That nigga Cam is known all around as a hard knock. Look what they did to him. They killed that nigga in tha public."

"Yeah Da, they up on some of my type shit. That's why we have to see this nigga Dirk. He's probably gangsta, but he ain't no damn fool. That nigga might roll Da. That's if he hasn't done it already. Here he comes now. Aight nigga, you just drive. I got this," Tex says, sliding into the backseat.

"Nigga, don't fuck my seats up. Wait until we get to the spot," Da tells him.

"What up Da Da? What up Tex?" Dirk says before entering the car.

"What's up homie?" Tex asks.

"Ain't shit," he says looking around nervously.

"What's the word on the streets, Dirk?"

"Man, the police have swept that shit under the rug."

That's exactly what Da Da and Tex are looking for Dirk to say.

They have already heard from a reliable source that he is talking to the homicide detective about unsolved cases. It is only a matter of time before Umar's case is one of them. Unknown to Da Da and Tex, the real snitch is Cam, who is already dead.

"Where we going Da Da?" Dirk asks as he pulls out of the Food Lion parking lot.

"Sit tight nigga, just ride."

"But I..." That's when he feels the cold steel from Tex's pistol.

"One word bitch, and I'll split yo' mothafuckin' wig. You think you can play both sides of the fence wit' two real niggas?"

All of Dirk's years in street justice flashes right before his eyes. He has made plenty of mistakes before and recovered. But he knows there is no recovery this time. *If I could just reach my gat* he thinks to himself. *These niggas think I'm a snitch.* Cam had scarred his name in the streets by spreading that rumor. He has the cops watching their every move. But as soon as Dirk found out, he had it stopped, trying to help the situation.

In reality, Dirk never knew anything about the stick-up. Cam had put him in on it without telling him what is going down. He knew Umar was a good dude, so after everything went down, he sent word to The Crew and Kiki that he knew nothing about the killing. Whether they believed him or not is irrelevant. It cleared his state of mind for that day. A scene he had already lived a thousand times. Everyday he chooses death before dishonor.

"The only bitches I know," says Dirk with a new burst of adrenaline, "is that snitch nigga Cam and the two bitches who couldn't face Umar face to face and shot him in tha ba..."

Boom! Brain matter and fragments hit the roof and front windshield.

"That's yo' bitch right there nigga!" Tex yells.

After dumping Dirk's body in a dumpster, they clean up the blood in Da Da's hooptie.

"Damn Tex, I told you to wait 'til we got on White Store Road."

"That nigga didn't wait 'til we got there to get slick, did he?"

"Well, make sure we clean all this shit up. I'll get a new windshield first thing Monday."

Beep. Beep. Beep. "Bout time this bitch got back at me."

"Who dat homie?"

"It's Terri, Da Da."

"What the fuck taking her so long to snag this nigga?"

"Chill homie. She says she needs a little more time. You said yo' self the nigga isn't slow."

"I am talkin' 'bout on the draw nigga."

"Whatever homie."

Terri has been hard at work trying to lure Q into her wrath. Q has come by on several occasions and Tee and El are either depositing money or picking up supplies at Sally's. Q stops by one evening after returning from seeing Kris in Charlotte. When he walks in, Terri has a client under the dryer. She glances through a new book called 'Little Ghetto Girl' by this chick outta Charlotte named Danielle Santiago.

"Hi, Q," Terri says in an overly eager voice.

"What's up Terri? Where's El and Tee?"

"They went to pick up supplies for the shop. You just missed them."

"Aight. I'm gonna use the office to make a call."

Q steps into the office to call Poo when the door opens and Terri walks in. Q has already peeped the game. He plays along with her until it becomes serious.

"Q, can I ask you a personal question?"

"I don't know, Terri. I try to keep personal things personal, ya' know?"

"Yeah, I understand," she says, turning to leave.

Grabbing her hand, he says, "Look Terri, I don't know you that well ma, but I know women. Whatever it is that's troubling you can be solved. You're a beautiful woman, Terri, a queen in my book. Don't settle for anything less than the best. I might not agree with the people you associate with, but that's your choice ma."

Q then pulls her into his muscular arms and whispers in her ear. "If there's anything you need taken care of, just ask."

Kissing her lightly on the lips, he releases her. "Now, to answer your question, no, me and Tee are not together, but we'll always be a part of each other's lives. She helped me through some rough times in my life. I owe her a lot. I'm willing to put everything on the line for her and anyone she considers a friend. Even you."

Q turns and walks right out of the office leaving her standing there, completely forgetting about his call.

From that point on, Terri fights with her inner feelings to no avail. She has fallen in love with her opposition. Left in the office all alone, Terri begins thinking *never have I melted in a man's arms that way. He showed so much compassion toward me. But why? I've never been told so many sweet things by a man before. Now I know why Tee could never totally free herself from him.* She knows from that moment on, she could never deceive him.

"W HAT'S UP T EX ?" T ERRI ASKS.

"I'm only touching bases with you on our situation. Wait, our situation? Nah ma, yo' situation. You said it would be a piece of cake Terri. Now tell me, what the fuck's going on?"

"I'm gonna need a little more time," she says, trying to stall Tex as long as she can.

"Look Terri, stop tha mothafuckin' games. I gave you fifteen Gs up front. Now it's on you how you get it done, but yo' ass better handle yo' business."

"Look Tex, you can have your money back if..."

"Look bitch, yo' ass in it to win it. I don't need no fifteen Gs. Ho, I need you. Get me Q or get yo' favorite dress out of the closet. Better yet, just lay anything out. Yo' shit's gonna be a closed casket anyway. You know my M.O. Terri. Nobody's safe, not even your child."

Hearing Lil' Ty's name makes Terri scream at the top of her lungs, "Don't fuck wit' my baby Tex. He's our child nigga."

"No Terri, he's yo' child. You have two weeks to come through. If not I will bleed yo' whole family." Click.

Terri is still holding the phone as if someone is on the other end. She knows Tex was a little strange when they met but would have never thought he would be so vicious. By the time the rumors of his line of work got back to her, it was too late. They were leaving the movie theater one night when Tex spotted one of his targets. He followed the man to his front door step, killing him before he could get his key in the door. To kill a man right in front of her like that, meant he thought no more of her than a four legged dog. After that, the abuse started until it was almost everyday. She was five months pregnant with little Ty when she left. She found a small apartment in Bennettsville, South Carolina, and stayed in hiding until Ty was born. She worked part-time and attended Chris Logan Hair School. That's where she met Tashonda. She had big dreams of owning her own salon someday. She had never met the guy Tashonda always talked about 24/7, but she knew he had to be special.

After graduating from school, Terri started working for a salon in South Carolina when Tashonda paged her and offered her a job. Once Tex found her, Ty was already walking. He talked her into letting his mother see his son. Terri was reluctant at first but finally gave in. She turned out to be very loving toward her only grandson. Terri and Tex never messed around again, but she being his baby-mama made him think he still had ownership.

Ty became ill with a severe case of bronchitis. Terri had no medical insurance, so she called Tex. Tex gave her the money saying that she owed him. Not thinking about anything but her son, she agreed to do what she had to do. When Tex finally told her what he wanted from her, Terri was stuck. Now, Tex has stooped so low that he offers to sacrifice his only son. What could one man have done to make another hate him with such a passion?

"May I speak to Q?"

"Yes, may I ask who's calling?"

"It's Terri from the shop Van, how are you?"

"I'm fine Terri... Well it's good talking to ya' here's Q".

"What's up Terri?" Q says looking back at Van giving her a wink. She smiles and says I love you.

"Hi, Q. I didn't mean to bother you but..."

"You don't have to say no more. Where are you?"

"At my apartment."

"I'm on the way. Are you alone?"

"Yes."

Hanging up the phone Q reaches for his coat.

"Van keep your cell phone line free ma, somethin's goin' on wit' Terri. I'm hopin' she comes clean, so we can eliminate the bullshit."

"Ok. Be careful babe."

As soon as Q steps inside Terri's door, she begins crying uncontrollably.

"Come on Terri, you gotta calm down ma. What's going on?"

She cries until Q's shirt is soaked from her tears. Q holds her close. "Terri talk to me. Does it have anything to do with your baby daddy?"

"It has a lot to do with him, Q."

"Well, start from the beginning."

After telling Q everything that is going on, he leans his head back and closes his eyes.

"I'm sorry, Q. I didn't have anybody else to turn to."

"Listen up, Terri. I don't blame you for anything. If you can't turn to your child's father for help then who else do you have? It takes a true sucker to drag his child's mother into something so serious and then to talk about murdering your own flesh and blood. Once you consider doing something as low as that, there's no turning back. I hate to see any child without their father. But Tex is going to die, Terri. I can't have no nigga walking around with that kind of hatred against me."

"What happened between you two to make Tex be willing to kill his own son?"

"You know ma, that's what makes it easy for me to gut this nigga. Until that night at the club, I had never seen Tex. The only thing it can be is envy. If he kills me, he thinks his street status will be sealed," Q explains. "Does Tex know where you live?" he asks.

"No, but I've been getting some strange phone calls."

"Okay, look, I have someone I want you to meet. He's my man Tim. Let me call him."

"Aight, but let me have that shirt to wash so your gurls won't be trippin'."

Q doesn't like undressing in front of her, but it will be hard explaining why he smells like Terri. "Yeah that's a damn good idea ma. I've already got enough problems." Pulling off his shirt, Q grabs Terri's cordless phone and begins calling Tim. "Yo I need you to come over to my people's house. The address is 3202 Erskine Dr."

"Aight, I'm on my way."

Terri is still standing behind him looking strangely at him when he places the receiver on its stand.

"What's the matter Terri?"

"Oh, I'm sorry. I, I…"

"You're gonna like my man," Q says, cutting her off before things get out of hand.

"I can't wait to meet him," she says while walking to the laundry room.

When Tim finally arrives, Q gives him the whole scoop on what's going on. Tim and Terri have only seen one another at the salon, but they click as soon as they are introduced.

"Yo, Terri, would it be aight if Tim stays here with you until we straighten this shit out?"

"It's cool. The spare bedroom is down the hall."

"Hold up homie, you know I got business on the set?"

"Yeah. That's why I'm calling June. He can take care of all the work for a few days."

"Big Kev and Corey got that nigga Young Jezzy up in that mothafucka tonight. You know that a nigga gotta roll up in that piece."

"You can still go nigga," Q says, walking through the door. Yelling over his shoulder, "Make sure you got Terri wit' you playboy."

Sitting on the couch, Tim grabs the remote control and begins flipping through the channels.

"Can I get you something to drink Tim?"

"Yeah, water will be cool ma."

Terri slips on a Baby Phat tank with matching shorts. When she returns, Tim notices that she has green eyes. *Damn this girl's fine.* He thinks to himself. *How can anybody wanna do any harm to something so beautiful?*

"So Terri, do they have a resident gym for the tenants here?"

"Yeah, it's on the other side of the complex, but it's nice."

"Do you work-out?"

"Sure," she says, standing up showing Tim her six-pack.

"That's nice, ma, but check this out," he says, raising his tank top. Tim is cut up nicely. No body fat anywhere. Terri is definitely impressed. They decide to go to the gym and work off some stress. After working out for a couple of hours, they go back to her apartment.

"So, Terri, when's the last time you been out ma?"

"I don't go out, Tim. I don't have time. When I'm off work, I spend most of my time with Lil' Ty. But he's been with his grandmother for two weeks. Now, I have to figure out how I'm going to bring him back home without running into Tex."

"Don't worry ma, we'll get your son back safely. But tonight, I'm taking you to our club. That cool?"

"Yeah, cool."

Chapter Nine

They Say It's The Life

By the time Q gets in touch with June, he had gotten pages from Asia and Big Kev. He calls Big Kev first. "What up homie?"

"What's good, Q?"

"Nothing much Kev. Sittin' here kickin' it wit' June and Pandora."

Pandora is June's girl from his hometown, Southeast D.C. She is a dime-piece. When Q had first seen her on The Block before he met June, he liked her style. He could tell by the short answers she gave him that she is loyal to her man.

"Me and Corey have to pick up Jezzy and his crew at the Charlotte Airport."

"Do you already have their rooms reserved?"

"Yeah homie, we got everything straight. Do you wanna ride? I can swing by and scoop you up."

"Aight Kev, but just meet me at The Club. I'll park my car there."

Q calls Asia while heading to The Club.

"Hi stranger," she says.

"What up, Babygirl?"

"You."

"Come on, stop playing ma."

"Okay Boo, it isn't that serious."

"It's not like that, ma. Just so much has been going on, that's all."

"Do you need me, Baby? I can be there in an hour."

"Well ma, I always need you. But right now, I have to meet Big Kev at The Club. We have to pick up the performers for tonight."

"The girls asked me if I'm coming tonight."

"Why not? Ya'll makin' all the money anyway," he says, laughing.

"I wish nigga. Are you coming back to Fayetteville with me tonight?"

"Only on one condition, and we'll discuss that at The Club."

"Anything you say Baby."

"Aight ma, I'll see you then."

Hanging up the phone, Q thinks about Van. She has always accepted his lifestyle. She knows about all the women. It comes along with the hustle game. She has put all her hopes and dreams in their relationship. He knows all the pimping will have to come to a stop soon. You can't be halfway out of the game; you have to give it all up.

Big Kev and Q rent a limo-van for Jezzy's entourage. After finally getting everybody situated, they head back to Rockingham. Q rides back with Big Kev, Jezzy, and his manager. He lays back in the cut while Big Kev discusses how the money will be exchanged. Jezzy's manager is pretty cool. He has a nice build up top. But if one of these country niggas hit that chin with those small ass legs he's walking on, it's lights out!

Jezzy has some New York chicks with him acting all stuck up and shit. One even calls Q a country boy and tells him to get her bags. Big Kev damn near falls over trying to get close enough before Q slaps the shit outta her ass. But just as smooth as she says it, he smoothly gives her a response. "You got the country boy part right, but this nigga don't do bags."

Before getting them another room, which is unnecessary to Q, they all want to check The Club setup out. As soon as they pull up at the club, Q can hear the same chick asking Big Kev about the drop-top blue 645 BMW sitting so close to the front door of The Club.

"That's that country boy you told to carry yo' bags."

"Word?"

"Word, Shawty."

Q takes Jezzy's bodyguards to Uriah's Fitness Center, for a much needed work out, then drops them back off to their private room.

"Yo' that is a good ass workout. Your man Uriah is the truth, homie."

"Yeah son, my shit's still on blow."

"Yo' someone will be here at 8:00 sharp to pick y'all up."

"Aight son."

Chapter Ten

Big Pimping

Everyone shows up at The Club. Jezzy's album is the hottest shit out. As usual, Q arrives late. The Club is already wall-to-wall. Q is very impressed with the security setup Corey and Poo have arranged. Fat Dave is at the dressing room door.

"What up, nigga?"

"What's up Q? Man everybody's looking for you homie. That nigga Yaro been asking when you is gonna get here." Yaro is Jezzy's manager. "He says as soon as you get here, holla at him."

Q knocks on the door of the dressing room. Yaro peeps out the door before opening it and letting Q inside. "What's up son? What took you so long to get here playa?"

"Had a few stops to make first," he says, giving Yaro a pound.

"Man, you country nigga's got it packed out there."

"Yea, we got like four towns in the house tonight."

"Yo, you got to make sure we get some of this small town pussy."

"You know I'm going to look out fam, but I got to go and make sure everything straight. So I'll holla at you after the show."

"No doubt".

Q leaves the room and starts on his way to the back office.

"What up Q?" says a cat outta Fayetteville named K-Love.

They have never had dealings before, but both are well respected in their hoods. K-Love hustles on a strip called The Murk AKA Murder Blvd. Q and Asia have stopped through Rudy's Pawn Shop a couple of times. Her cousin Cream works there on weekdays. Q met K-Love there, and they became cool.

"K-Love, what up nigga? I see you're still living up to your name homie," he says, eyeing the two females on his arms.

"Nah Q, both of them like Jezzy and they both love me," he says laughing.

"Nigga, you a pimp to your heart. Enjoy the show playa. Holla." Walking toward the door, Q feels someone reach out and slide a cube of ice down his shirt. It's two of his homegirls from The Grove.

"Damn Angie, you tryin' to freeze a nigga, huh?"

"Yeah nigga, then maybe I'll get to thaw yo' ass out," she says giving him a hug and kiss.

"Save some for me," says his other homegirl Marie.

"What's up?" he says, taking them both in his arms. "Ya'll aight?"

"Yeah, we're just waitin' on the show to start."

"It should be startin' in a few. Go to the bar and tell Aileen it's on your big bro. Food, drinks, whatever."

"Aight nigga, but one day you'll give in," she says sticking her bottom lip out. Angie and Marie have grown up since the days in the neighborhood. Both are phat to death, but Q always looks at them as his little sisters. Plus, Van would kill his mothafuckin' ass. They are all like family.

After getting his cola from the bar, Q steps into the office. Corey is sitting at the poker table with at least seven strippers lounging in chairs around him. Asia is sitting behind the office desk looking like a china doll. *Yeah I'm making that trip to Fayetteville early tonight* Q thinks to himself. At first Asia wouldn't show her feelings in front of the other girls. But after Q started laying that lumber, she quickly changed that hide-and-seek shit to just seek.

"What's up everybody?" he says, heading for the desk.

"Hi Q," everyone says, speaking at once. Asia stands and gives him a hug.

"Mmmm.. Mmm. I missed you, Q."

"I missed you too, ma," he says, patting her left ass cheek.

"Can we leave now?" Asia says, hearing the other girls whispering in the background.

"Not right now baby, but as soon as the shows over, I'll be ready to bounce. And don't worry about none of that shit you hearing over there ma. You know me. Hell, you just got lucky yourself."

Bap... Bap. She gives him a two piece.

"Aight ma, you know I'm just kidding, come here."

Q doesn't watch many of the shows they have but when Jezzy comes out and gets on the mic, his voice controls the whole crowd. Q steps out of the office and heads to his private table. When he gets there, it is already occupied. Tee and Elbony are screaming and dancing to Jezzy's rhymes while Tim has about five inches of tongue down Terri's throat. He eases up behind Tee and puts his arm around her waist. She turns and gives him a much needed kiss.

"Hey baby."

"Hmmmm, you taste good," she says, giving him another kiss.

"Why haven't you called me all weekend Q? You're getting slack mister."

"I promise I'll make it up to you real soon."

"It better be soon, nigga. You haven't changed my oil, rotated my tires or nothin'. And I'm in dyin' need of a tune-up," she says.

"Baby, don't forget where we're at," he says.

"They look busy to me Boo." Tim is still hung in Terri's throat.

"Damn Tee, let me pull this nigga up outta this girl before he kill her."

"Hurry back, so you can kill me," she says with a wicked grin on her face.

"Damn nigga, that shit look like it might hurt," Q says, sitting right beside them at his table. They are both caught by surprise and try to pull apart, but as deep as they were in each other's mouths it is already too late. "Busted."

"Wha... What up Q? When did you get here?"

"I been sittin' here for fifteen minutes watching you homie. I see both of you have gotten acquainted."

"Yeah. She good peoples homie."

"I told you that before you met her T. So, do I have to get someone else to watch her for the next few days?"

"Nah homie, I got this," he says, squeezing her hand.

"Aight T," Q says, pulling him close.

"Look, I'm a slide to the Ville until late tomorrow afternoon, so make sure Tee and El's straight."

"No problem, homie."

The dance floor is shoulder to shoulder. Q pulls Tee and El onto the dance floor rocking while Tim and Terri fight to keep their hands off each other. When the show is over, Q walks Tee and El to her car. Tee looks at Q.

"Baby, what time will you be there? Do you want anything to eat?"

"Nah, ma. I probably won't make it until tomorrow anyway."

"What?"

"Come on Tee, you know we have to count the bar and booth. Then somebody has to clean this place up."

"Q, it's not like you can't get nobody to take care of the cleaning."

"Aight ma, I'll be there as soon as we get the money counted. Cool?"

"I love you," she says before pulling off. Q stands there knowing he has been defeated. *Damn, there goes my trip to Fayetteville* he thinks.

After leaving the club, Terri and Tim pull up at Shoney's restaurant to grab something to eat. After eating, they go to Tim's house on Midway Road.

"Make yourself at home while I check these messages." He gives her one of his nylon undershirts and shorts to put on after she showers.

"Everything else is in the bathroom, Shawty." Tim checks his messages and then he showers and heads for the couch. Terri lays on his bed half asleep. Tim flips through the channels on his 52" plasma screen. A little while after dozing off, he is suddenly awakened by Terri's voice.

"Is this the way you treat all your company?"

"Nah ma, I just thought..."

"Well, maybe you should leave the thinking to me," she says, standing in front of his TV screen.

Tim can see the outline of her body as she walks toward him. She lays between his legs with her head on his stomach. Tim fights hard to control his erection. He tries pulling her up to him by her shoulders. "Come here ma."

"But I'm comfortable right here, baby," she says, catching on to what he is trying to do.

Looking up at him with those green eyes is all he can take. Tim watches TV as much as he can.

Chapter Eleven

Working Overtime

It is 5:30 a.m. Sunday when Q grabs his keys off the hotel nightstand. Asia is snoring lightly. There's no use trying to sneak out, so he nudges her shoulder.

"Wake up ma, wake up."

"Humm, what time is it Q?"

"It's 5:30 am. We already discussed what time I'm leaving."

"Yeah, I know Boo, but can I at least have a kiss?"

"Ain't no question Shawty, come 'ere." Q massages Asia's breast with both hands, teasing her.

"Baby, what if I were to ever ask you to stop dancing?" he asks, not knowing where the question came from.

"Boo, I'll do anything you ask, just don't stop massaging me?" she says, now moaning.

"I'm serious, Shawty. Have you ever thought about quitting?"

Opening her eyes, she looks at him. "Q, I've already stopped dancing. I quit over two months ago. The only time I'm with the girls is when we come to The Club. I've been meaning to tell you, but I didn't want you to think I had quit because I... hmmmm."

"Tell me, Asia," he says, easing his way down to her navel. She moans his name one last time before collapsing back on the bed.

"'Cause I'm in love with you baby. I love you."

"That's all I wanted to hear," Q says jokingly. "We're gonna have to finish this another time. You know I got love for you too right?"

"Yea, baby I know."

"I will call you later."

Q arrives at Tee's townhouse just before 6:00 a.m. Still dark, he thinks to himself, *maybe Tee's fallen asleep.* Putting his phone on vibrate, he slowly turns the key. He makes it inside quietly, but it doesn't make a difference. Tee is lying on the couch in one of those sexy tank tops. She looks like a giant black Barbie doll. Going to the shower, he tries not to wake her. He steps into the shower and instantly begins to feel energized. The water soothes his skin. Q closes his eyes and relaxes for the next half hour. After drying off, he walks back into the den. Tee is still asleep. Q walks around to the front of the couch and kneels down in front of her. He bends over and kisses her toes lightly, then her ankles. When he gets to her calves, he has her attention.

"Baby, when did you get here?" she says, never opening her eyes.

"About an hour ago," he says.

"Hmmm, you smell good ma." Tee can't respond.

Chapter Twelve

Sacrifices

The holidays are almost over. The Crew is once again back in the saddle. The only drama that has jumped off is the discovery of Dirk's body in a dumpster outside the Boro. The news is not shocking to The Crew. They receive several messages from his people saying he knew nothing of the stick-up, and he had sent his own mother to Kiki's house to tell her he had nothing to do with it. Dirk did everything to clear his name. Every Crew member knew Dirk wasn't lying. He would have never sacrificed his mother by sending her to what he knew was a killing ground. She came only because of a mother's love for her son, not caring about the dangers. The sad part is that by the time The Crew gets the messages, Dirk is already dead. Q is at home when he gets the call from June about Dirk's murder.

"Sit tight June. I'm on my way through."

"Aight homie, check The Grill if I'm not on the set."

Van is in her study on the computer. "Baby, I'm going to meet June down on The Block. Do you wanna come?" he asks her.

"Yes, Baby. That will save me an extra trip downtown."

"Van, I know how your trips downtown are. We'll end up spending all day in one store ma."

"It won't take long to pay a couple bills," she says, going into the bedroom to get dressed. The temperature is close to 65 degrees outside. It is a beautiful day.

"Grab your leather coat ma," Q yells, heading out to the garage.

"What? What do I need my leather co…" The sounds of Q's bike drowns out her words. When Van steps out the house, she has on some tight jeans, Timberland boots, and her leather coat.

Q winks at her. "So, you ready to ride Bonnie?"

"Yea Clyde," she says, climbing on behind him.

Van loves riding behind him, especially on long trips like to the beach. When they arrive uptown, Q and June stand in front of The Grill and talk. He can see Van across the street talking with someone she went to school with.

"Has anybody gone by to see if Mrs. Watson needs anything, June?"

"Nah Q, not yet, but The Crew plans on paying their respects soon. We think we'll give the family time to get situated with all the arrangements. Dirk's a soldier."

"Yea, you right June, he is. I am willing to bet my life on it. Dirk stayed true to the end. It's fucked up the police are already claiming it's a drug deal gone bad."

Q and June both know who the killers are. They murdered Dirk thinking he would talk. Dirk and Cam are the only ones who could link them to Umar's murder. With them out of the way, the murderers would be in the clear in the eyes of the police, but in Q's eyes they are living on borrowed time.

"Yo, me and Van are going to go ahead and swing by there."

"Aight fam, we holla at you later."

When Q and Van arrive at Dirk's mother's house, friends and family are everywhere. Van is kind of tensed up from all the staring.

"It's ok, ma," he says, rubbing her neck. "They all good peoples. They just lost one of their family members for nothing. I can feel their pain."

Q and Van enter the house and find Mrs. Watson alone in her living room.

"Come on in, son," she says. "You and the lil' lady have a seat."

She is holding a baby picture of Dirk in her hands. "He is a good boy," she says with tears now flowing. "I begged Dee everyday to get out those streets. He tried so hard to get his life on the right track, but the streets always seemed to win. That boy Cam is nothing but trouble, son. Dirk never knew anything about what happened to that poor child Umar. I had to threaten him several times not to leave and come straight to Umar's family and get this mess straight. I know when someone loses a loved one, sometimes they react before thinking."

Q speaks, "Mrs. Watson, we know Dirk didn't have anything to do with Umar's death. Cam put a bad name on him. Mrs. Watson, do you know if the police have any suspects?"

"No, son, but I'm a wise old lady now. I've been blessed with plenty of wisdom," she says, now standing. "The streets have been talking for years. I asked God to send me the answers I'm looking for with my son's death. I begged him not to let his life be taken in vain. As soon as I got off my knees, you walked in, so now you can tell me who killed my son."

Q stands there speechless. He is never very good when it comes to his elders. He could never understand how they always knew something before you told them.

"Mrs. Watson," Van says, "we have a pretty good idea who is behind Dirk's death. But, it's just our own theory, and we don't deal with cops."

"I understand my child. There's too many problems with the police. Besides, I believe in an eye for an eye. Whoever killed him deserves nothing less than Dirk got. I'm not gonna come out and ask you to do anything to jeopardize your lives, but I ask only one favor. If by chance you happen to run into who did this to my baby, tell them to give my son this message: "Mama sends her love." With that, she breaks down crying in Q's arms.

After leaving Dirk's mother's house, Q and Van make a few stops downtown. They sit in one of their favorite eating spots, the Peking-Wok Chinese Restaurant. Q stares across the table at Van. He wonders, *why am I so blessed to have her? She could have any man she wants, but she chooses me. But why? I don't deserve something so special.* So, he says to her, "Baby Girl, thanks for saving me at Dirk's moms. I... I..."

Van cut him off, "Q, when someone requests something from you, they're requesting it from me too. We're one, remember?"

She smiles then says, "'I' doesn't come before 'we' with us. Whichever way you decide to handle this situation, handle it with an iron hand. I'm behind you 100%. Now stop staring at me and eat," she says, handing him an egg roll.

Chapter Thirteen

The Game Keeps Pulling Me Back

Terri and Tim's relationship blossoms into something special for the both of them. All of their time is spent together; they are becoming inseparable. Q would tease Tim about Terri saying how he should put a ring on her finger because she is wifey material. Tim, on the other hand, can't agree more. In reality, Tim understood where Q was coming from

"What's the matter ma? You've been quiet all day."

Truth is, Terri has been depressed the last few days. "Come on, talk to me Terri. What is it?" Tim asks.

"It's my son, Tim. I haven't seen him in almost four weeks now. I have to do something before Tex does something stupid."

"Aight ma, get your coat."

"What?"

"Get your coat, ma. We have to pick up your son."

Tim and Terri leave without calling any of The Crew. Terri calls Tee at the shop to let her know she will be late coming in. "Hi Tee."

"Hey stranger! I haven't heard from you since you left work Thursday. Your clients have been calling everyday worrying about you."

"It's only been three days. I'll be a little late today, but I should make it before twelve."

"Okay, since you're the boss now, Miss Thang. I'll make your appointments after twelve," says Tee, sounding sarcastic.

"Don't say it like that Tee. You know I don't mean it like that."

"Just messin' wit' you gurl. Now hurry up and get here before I decide to fire you."

"Aight gurl, as soon as I drop Lil Ty off at the daycare."

"What? You have Lil' Ty?" she asks, sounding excited. "Bring him with you. My appointments will be finished for the day. I will..."

"Wait a minute, Tee. I don't have him yet. I'm on my way to pick him up."

"Terri, look. Don't go there alone. It's too dangerous."

"I'm not alone, Tee. Tim's with me."

"Don't you think you should've let someone know before you just took off like that?"

"Yeah, you're right Tee, but Tim insisted on not calling any of The Crew."

"Aight, but if I don't hear from you in one hour I'm calling Q and June."

"Okay, but we should be back sooner than that."

"Aight, be safe."

The ride to Wadesboro goes smoothly. They make it safely to Tex's mother's house. Lil' Ty is thrilled to see his mother. Mrs. Johnson is visibly shaken by something. She rushes to pack Lil' Ty's night bag while trying to button his jacket up all at once.

Terri asks, "Is everything okay Mrs. Johnson?"

"Yes, my child, but..."

Tim cuts her off. "But your son's on the way over, huh?"

"Yes, and he's ..."

Tim dashes for the door to retrieve his gun.

The door closes behind him.

Terri talks again to Mrs. Johnson, "Mrs. Johnson, why didn't you tell me this on the phone?"

Mrs. Johnson says through tears and a lot of shame, "Because my only son had a pistol to my head. He says he would kill me and my grandbaby if I said anything."

Terri gets up to call the police. A long volley of shots ring outside in front of the house.

"Tim!" Terri screams, running for the front door. Outside, she sees Tex and Da Da standing over Tim's body. They each shoot him one more time in his back as he lies lifelessly on the ground.

"No... No... Nooooo!" Terri screams, running towards Tim.

Tex raises his gun and fires. Click. Click. Click. He has run out of bullets.

"Come on Tex! Five-o will be here in a minute!" Da Da screams.

"Aight, nigga let me load this mothafu..." Tex cut short his words as he hears the loud blasting of sirens.

"Tex, let's bounce man."

Mrs. Johnson has called 911. When they arrive, paramedics try to pry Terri away from Tim. Her clothes are soaked with blood. After expecting a D.O.A., they miraculously find a small pulse in Tim's body. They rush him to Wadesboro Medical, and then transfer him to Charlotte Presbyterian Hospital.

Terri is right by his side talking to her Baby. "Tim, stay here with me Boo. Don't leave me here all alone. I can't make it without you."

"Keep talking to him young lady," says the paramedic.

Tim loses so much blood, it will be a miracle for him to survive. Lil' Ty leaves his grandmother's house as Terri instructed before leaving with the paramedics. The police are told to take him straight to Honey's Beauty Salon to a Tashonda Davis.

Tee can't figure out what is tugging at her insides so much. "What is it?" she says to herself. The clock read 11:58 a.m. Terri hasn't shown up yet. Three of her clients are already there. Tee contemplates on calling Q. *Maybe I'm overreacting* she thinks. Lost in her own thoughts, Tee is startled by someone banging on the door.

"Tee, Tee." It's El. Rushing to the door, Tee snatches it open.

"What's wrong El? Wh..."

"The police are out front," she says, interrupting her. "They are asking for you."

Running from her office, she finds two officers standing inside her lobby area. "Are you Tashonda Davis?" they ask her. Tee just stands there numb. "Excuse me Miss, but are you Tashonda Davis?"

"Uh, uh... Yes, I am," she says barely above a whisper.

"Can we speak to you in private?" the officer asks, looking around the lobby.

"Yes. Yes, please step into my office."

After closing the door,they waste no time. "Mrs. Davis, there's been an accident. Do you know a Terri Eberhart?"

"Yes sir, I do, officer. What's going on?"

"Miss Davis, we were instructed to bring Tyler Eberhart to you from his mother."

"Officer, please tell me what the hell's going on!" she demands, getting hysterical.

"There's been a shooting, Miss Davis. Do you know Timothy Gregory?"

When Tee hears Tim's real name, she knows it's bad. "Yes, I know him," she says between sobs.

"Calm down. You have to be strong for this child." Elbony brings Lil' Ty into the office. He holds both hands out, reaching for Tee.

I have to be strong, she thinks. *I have to be.*

The officers give Tee all the details about Tim's shooting. Their last report is that he has been transported to Wadesboro Hospital. He was shot several times, and has lost a lot of blood. His chances of survival are slim.

After the officers leave, Tee texts Q, putting in her code. Then she does the same with June and the rest of The Crew. Everyone calls right back and are on the way over, except Q. He hasn't returned her call, which causes her even more worry. Big Kev is the last to arrive, but still no word from Q.

Elbony deals with the clients as best she can. Tee sets later dates for Terri's clients. They are very loyal to her and understand because she has a good work ethic.

Everyone sits in the back office. June speaks first. "Tee, what's going on, ma? And where are Q and Tim?"

Tee begins to sob lightly, and then speaks, "I don't know where Q's at, but Tim's been shot."

"SHOT!" everyone yells at the same time. "What, where, who?"

"I don't know," she responds. "But it happened in Wadesboro."

Poo speaks up, "What tha fuck is Tim doing in the Boro' without anybody knowing?"

Tee responds, "He didn't want any of The Crew involved, but Terri called the salon and said she would be a little late. Then she told me that Tim was taking her to pick up her son."

Big Kev opens his cell and dials Van and Q's home number.

"Hello," Van answers on the first ring. "What up, Sis? It's Kev."

"Kev, what's going on?"

"It's bad Lil' Sis. It's really, really bad. Where's Q, I need to speak with him."

"He's out at the kennel working Skull on the treadmill. Now, tell me what's going on Kev?"

"Tim's been shot, ma. That's all I know right now. He barely had a pulse when he left the scene. He's lost a lot of blood. They give him almost no chance to survive."

"Don't leave us Tim," she says sobbing on the other end of the phone, as if talking to him.

"Ma, you have to get Q. Everyone else is at the salon."

She responds, "I'm on the way now, Kev. Q's cell phones are here, so I have to go to the kennel."

Grabbing her keys, she jumps in Q's Mustang. Big Kev calls her on her cell again, telling her everything else he knows about the situation.

"Damn Van, slow that shit down." He can hear her going through the gear box of Q's 'Stang.

Over at the kennel, Q is working Skull for his championship match. He works him up to three hours on the mill.

"Come on boy, only twenty more minutes," he says.

Skull loves to work. At 52 pounds match weight, he is a dead serious and a straightforward type of bulldog that never stops coming. After putting Skull back on his chain, Q cleans some of the puppy kennels. He is really starting to enjoy his life outside The Game. Looking around, he gives thanks and counts his blessings. The sound of a roaring engine breaks his thoughts. It's a familiar roar. It sounds so familiar to Q that he doesn't realize it's his own car until Van barely makes the curve.

"What the fu..." he says to himself. Van slides to a stop then jumps out screaming his name. Dropping the water hose, Q runs to her aid. She falls into his arms. Unable to understand her, he tries to calm her down.

"Wait a minute Boo," he says, grabbing her hands. Still unable to calm her, he tightens his grip. Van screams.

"What's wrong?" says Q.

"It's... it's... it's Tim, Q. It's Tim!"

"What about Tim, Boo?"

"He's been shot, Q! He's been shot!"

Taking her by one hand, he runs to the car. Van tries to explain what happened as best she can on the way to the salon. Q doesn't say one word all the way there. All you can smell throughout the car is the clutch burning. When Q and Van enter the salon, everybody is still in the back office.

"What happened? What the fuck happened?" he demands as he enters the office.

Tee explains what the police have told her about the shooting. The Crew has never seen Q this upset before. He is pacing back and forth with tears in his eyes.

He finally says, "Kev, June, everybody, let's roll. Tee you take Lil' Ty home and wait for our call." He looks at Van. It's her first time in Tee's salon. He can see she feels out of place.

"It's okay ma, I got you," he says, guiding her out of the salon.

The Crew races up Hwy 74 towards Wadesboro Hospital. Q reaches over and rubs Vans hand. His thoughts turn to his homie Tim. *Why didn't he let someone know he was making a move like that?*

He knew Tim could be stubborn sometimes but something or somebody had to distract him for someone to get the ups on him like that. Q knows Tim is too streetwise to be caught slipping. Q has already lost some good people to this Game. Now, there is a strong possibility he has lost another. He vows right then that if he loses any more family in these streets, it would not be by anyone involved in Tim's death. They will long be dead!!!

Chapter Fourteen

Loyalty

When they arrive at Wadesboro Hospital, they brace themselves for the worst. After being held in the waiting room for an hour or more, someone finally informs them that Tim has been air-lifted to Presbyterian Hospital. They ride for another hour and a half, not knowing whether their comrade is still living or dead. They arrive to some good and bad news. Tim is still alive, but barely. He has to be operated on immediately and given a blood transfusion. The doctors gave him a 60/40 chance of survival.

Van finds Terri in one of the waiting rooms close to the operating room. She still has on the blood soaked clothes from the scene. Her head is in her lap as she cries and prays not to lose Tim. Tears are now flowing from Van's eyes as she kneels in front of Terri. They embrace, trying to comfort each other. Q and June talk with the doctor who is treating Tim.

The doctor says, "I'm sorry about what happened to your friend. The only good news I can offer to you is the fact that he's still alive. But I have to be frank with both of you. The worst is yet to come. You see, Timothy's in the early stages of a long, long battle for his life. The operation went well, but the loss of so much blood concerns me more than anything. He was shot eight times from behind..."

Q interrupts the doctor. "Excuse me Doc, but did you say he was shot from behind?"

"Yes son, he was shot six times from a distance of more than twenty feet. Two other shots were close range, still from behind. Those two were so close to the spinal cord, we decided not to attempt to remove them. If you have a number I can reach you in case..."

"We'll be in the waiting room, Doc," Q says, turning to leave. "That will be fine," the doctor says. "Someone will keep you informed on an hourly basis. Can I ask one more question before you leave sir?"

Q responds, "Anything Doc?"

"Well, Timothy was shot eight times from behind, that we all know. The puzzling part during the operation was that I removed two different cartridges from his body. He had three nine millimeter bullets and two forty caliber bullets. One's caliber is undetermined because of its damage. Then, they're two still in his back. He's a lucky young man to be in I.C.U. instead of the morgue. So it makes me wonder... How many people were there?"

After speaking with the doctor, June and Q return to the waiting room to give the rest of The Crew the news. They all take it hard. Van walks up with a blood-soaked Terri. Both of their faces bear the pain they feel for their friend. Big Kev grabs them both, trying to comfort them.

June speaks, "Yo Q, this shit's bad homie, real bad."

"Yeah, you're right June." He can barely control his rage. "Let's just concentrate on Tim right now, homie. We owe him that."

"You right, homie. But I hope you're thinking what I'm thinking."

"Fam, you one of the realest niggas I've ever met. But to be truthful, your mind can't even register the pain and wrath that's about to be dealt."

Tim made it the first two days on what the doctors called sheer heart. "He's a pretty determined young man," the doctor says.

Van takes Terri to a mall and hotel close by, so that she can get herself together. Before this, she never left Tim's side. Q keeps Tee up on Tim's condition by phone. She hates the fact that she is the only one not there. Q assures her she can come in the next couple days. Sitting in the cafeteria, Q got some much needed time alone with Van.

"Ma, how's Terri holding up?"

"She's holding on as best she can Q, but if she loses Tim, I don't think she'll make it."

"Yeah, I feel you. I don't think any of us will."

"Q, I took a few days off work, but I have to go in on Wednesday. My boss says my patients aren't eating well. They're asking for me daily."

"Aight ma, you drive yourself back tonight. Get some rest, but make sure you call me as soon as you're safely at home. Big Kev, Poo, Corey, and Dave will follow you back. Can you talk Terri into going home and getting some rest?"

"Baby, I've tried everything possible. She refuses to leave his side."

"Okay. You better be getting back," he says, hugging her tightly. "Oh yeah, one more thing, Shawty. Look in our closet and blow the dust off his brother," he says patting under his left arm.

She nods slowly in agreement with what is to come. "I love you baby. Be safe and come home to me. Remember, they showed Tim no mercy, even though you let them live twice. Don't let it be a third time."

"It won't be Shawty, it won't be. Call me."

"One."

Q steps into Tim's room after Van leaves. Terri is sitting in the same spot she has been in for the past two days. He hasn't spoken to her since the accident. Walking up behind her, he places a hand on her shoulder.

She looks up and says, "I'm sorry Q. It's all my fault. If we hadn't..."

"Wait a minute, Terri," Q says. "It's not your fault. Tim has a good heart. He will help anybody out in the same situation. He'll be Aight Shawty, trust me. If God didn't have a plan for him, he would have taken him that day. Now com' on, let's get something to eat before Tim wakes up and thinks you're a skeleton or some shit." Before she could protest, Q has her by the hand leading her out the door.

While waiting for their food to arrive, he asks her if she feels like talking about what happened.

She agrees, the sooner the better she figures. After telling Q everything she knows, he asks her over and over about Tex's mother and her involvement. She assures Q that Mrs. Johnson had nothing to do with the shooting.

"I really think her life's in danger, Q. He put a pistol to his own mother's head!"

He is a cold nigga. Q has to admit that. "Aight ma, let's eat and get back to our man."

On the third and fourth day, Tim's condition takes a turn for the worse. The doctors think they are going to lose him, but he fights for his life.

On the first day of the second week, he almost gives Terri a heart attack when he squeezes her hand tightly. "Tim, you have to wake up, so we can go home Boo. The Crew has been asking for you every day. I haven't been to work in almost two weeks, baby."

Terri has been talking to Tim every day since the accident. She holds his hand almost twenty four hours a day. But on this particular day, she combs out his braids while talking to him about the things they need to get done once they get home.

"Tim, we have to get you some clothes up here to wear outta this place." Terri drops her comb and bends over to pick it up. "OUCH!" she says, not realizing what has happened. "What are you trying to do, break my fingers or something Boo."

Then it hits her. "Oh my God," Terri says, stumbling backwards into the empty food trays. She runs and gets the nurses. They ask her to speak to him again. "Tim, if you can hear me, Baby, squeeze my hand." No response.

After she repeats this several more times, the doctor and nurses are about to give up and say it's just his nerves. Terri says one more thing. "Tim, I love you with all my mind, body, and soul. You don't have to respond Boo, I know you can hear me." Tim squeezes her hand so tight, she has to almost pry it loose. Terri is in tears.

The doctors say he is already a miracle. Tim is on his long road to recovery. The Crew gets excited over the news. Q can only sit and cry when he hears the news. He has not been the same person since all this happened.

Tee drives up on Thursday morning. She enters Tim's room for the first time. Terri lies beside him on his bed with tears slowly rolling down her cheeks. Walking over, Tee pulls the hair back from Terri's face then speaks to her. "Terri, wake up. It's your boss and you're fired."

Climbing off the bed, they hug each other. "What, have you forgotten about all of us back home?" says Tee.

"No gurl, you know better."

Turning serious, Tee asks, "How is he?"

"Why don't you ask for yourself?" says Terri, reaching for Tim's hand.

"No Terri, I ca..."

"Just say hi to him, Tee. You don't think he misses you too?"

"T...T...Tim? It's me, Tee. Can you hear me?" He squeezes her hand giving her an answer. She looks back at Terri in amazement. "He can hear me ,Terri!"

"Yes, he sure can gurl! He's also told me he'll be waking up soon."

Tee looks back at Tim. "Well, get you some sleep Lil' Brother," she says, kissing his forehead. "I love you." When Tim hears the words "I love you" he squeezes down tightly on Tee's hand. "OUCH!" she says shockingly.

"Oh, I forgot to tell you about the 'I love you' subject. He's very sensitive to those words," she says smiling.

"I see that now," Tee says, rubbing her hand.

Tee and Terri talk about Lil' Ty and the salon for most of the day. "You know Terri, your clients are some of the most loyal people I've ever seen. They won't let me or El do no more than wash their hair. Mrs. Alsbrook's perm has been gone for two weeks, but she won't let anyone touch her hair. She looks like a chicken!" Tee says, making them both laugh.

Tim hears everybody's voice that comes into his darkness as it seems he is trapped in his own world, just lying peacefully on what feels like a cloud, Whenever someone tells him to wake up, he raises himself up and walks toward a light that seems to be right in front of him. Only the light seems to have legs of its own. A familiar voice enters his darkness as he lies on his cloud.

It says to him, "Tim, I got out of The Game because of this very reason. I lost Umar over nothing. I almost lost you the same way, but you're blessed with another chance. There are many people here who love you, homie. Everybody's fingers are crossed except mine. Cause I know in my heart that you're coming home. You and a few others are the only ones who know my colt had a brother, but it's time that a lot more get to meet him. Whenever you decide to wake up, have Terri page me homie. Oh yeah, you better marry her homie. She wifey material."

"Wait! Wait! Don't leave, homie. Take me with you."

"In due time, my son," another voice says. "In due time."

Chapter Fifteen

Dreaming Of the Get Back

June and Q ride through Wadesboro coming from Charlotte. After stopping by the mall to see his friend, Kris, they head back to Rockingham. Coming through The Boro', they come up on Salisbury Street and go straight into creep mode.

"Man, I oughta light this whole mothafuckin' block up," says June.

Q tells him to pull over into a parking lot. Q usually doesn't let his cockiness guide his intentions, but he's been feeling like the old Q lately. They pull into the Mini-Mart's parking lot. There is a group of women standing at the payphone.

"Yo' watch my back homie," says Q.

"I'm a holla at these hoes. If you see anything funny, wake Mac up nigga."

"Aight homie, but you better be duckin' 'cause I'm killin', bitches and all."

Q walks up to the girls. "What's up Dina, Neese, and you..."

"My name is whatever you want it to be," the third girl says, giving him her hand.

"Aight Shawty, I'll just call you mine from now on. But you can call me Q." She smiles from ear to ear. "Dina, can I holla at you for a minute?" asks Q.

"Sure. Excuse me y'all," she says, eyeing the chick without a name the most.

"Yo' look Dina..."

"Look Dina my ass Q," she says. "Why you tryin' to push up on that bitch in front of me?"

"Damn Dina, stop trippin', you know I'm only fuckin' wit' her. Anyway, what's good?" Q says, patting her on the ass.

"Oh, nothin'," she says, now sounding all sweet and shit.

"Look I need a favor from you, ma."

"Anything you need, just let me know Q. I got you."

"Aight ma, page me any time after nine and make sure you already got the room. You need money?"

"Nah, I'm straight, Baby."

"Aight. Get at me." With that said, he walks by the other two girls giving them a wink and a nod. *Damn that bitch do got a fat ass* he thinks, looking back.

Jumping back into the car, he notices June has laid both clips out on the seat. "Damn nigga, you going to war or some shit?"

"Just as soon as you give me the green light nigga, I'm a sit down on this whole mothafuckin' spot."

"It won't be long now, homie. I just got the ball rolling. Them two nigga's ridin' high right now, but when it go down all this Boro shit gonna be hip to The P.G. Crew."

Within the first two weeks, the news of Tim's shooting becomes old news. Tex and Da Da have been on the low since the shooting. Besides, the police aren't crazy. They know whoever it was that did the shooting doesn't give a fuck about killing again. They would make a few bogus reports then fake like they actually looked for a mothafucka. But all Tex and Da Da want is eight hours. Eight trouble free hours. They know Tim is already dead. No one could live through that many shots. Then, the two wet tee-shirts they gave him at close range put the icing on the cake.

"Da Da, it's been two weeks nigga. Let's roll. That shit's old news now duke," Tex points out.

"Yeah, it's probably cooled down by now. At least the cops won't be harassing our asses. That's unless your mother told them something."

"That's why you should've let me smoke her ass. Her and that bitch."

"Tex, you're a cold blooded mothafucka. What kinda person would kill his child's mother, not to mention his own?"

"I'll tell you what kind Da Da. The kinda nigga who's already been to hell and back. I'm twenty nine years old nigga. The odds had me never making twenty. So, I'm nine to the good. If my mother told the police anything, then she's against me. If you're against me, then you're my enemy. I don't give a fuck who you are. I'm a lay yo' ass down."

Tex and Da Da ride through their set, Salisbury Street. Business is looking a little slow for a Thursday. Females are always walking up and down the street trying to catch the attention of a baller coming through.

"Damn Tex, shit looks dead around here. Did you give that joint to Dex?"

"Yeah Da, I gave him the whole thing homie. He paged me two hours ago and says money is flowin'."

"Flowin'? Nigga, this shit look dead to me."

"Maybe the jump-out rode through on the runners. Pull over at the Mini-Mart, Da Da. I see that nigga Ham talking to Shea, Dina, and Neese."

They both jump out the car. Da Da runs inside the store while Tex hollers at Ham. "What up my nigga, you Aight?"

Ham looks around all nervous and shit. "What up Tex?" he says, still looking suspicious.

"What's the matter with you nigga? Five-o been through here or something? You look like you seen a ghost, homie."

"Man, you just missed them two cats from Rockingham."

"WHAT?!? Them two niggas stopped on our shit?"

"Yeah, homie. Them two niggas creeped through this bitch like they want war Tex. They stopped right here and that big nigga jumped out like he owned this mothafucka."

"Who did he talk to?" Tex asks Ham.

"He spoke to Dina, Neese, and Shea."

The girls are still standing at the phone booth. Dina hates Tex with a passion. Her brother was murdered in cold blood in front of at least twenty people who wouldn't come forward and point out his killer.

Everyone knows it was done by the nigga known as "Tex" around The Boro. The cops only need one witness to make an arrest, but still no one has come forward. Dina is still furious. She hates nothing more than a coward. She confronted Tex one day on her own, calling him a murderer, vowing one day to get even.

"That damn Dina's gettin' on my nerves, Da Da. She's been sending little fucked up messages about her brother's murder through Shea."

"Fuck that bitch, Tex. She doesn't got any proof about Bolo's death."

"Aight Da, but if she keep on stressing a nigga 'bout that dumb shit, I'm a see to it she be dealt wit'."

Da Da and Tex make their quick exit from the Mini-Mart parking lot after hearing about June and Q. After seeing Tex and Da Da come through, just like always, she feels the pain of her brother's death all over again, a pain that can only be relieved by her thirst for revenge. After getting the room, she pages Q and puts the room number in his pager. She showers and lies across the bed and goes to sleep.

Q drops June off on The Block. He has a couple more stops to make before he can meet Van for lunch. He pulls into the salon's parking lot at about 10:30 a.m. It's already crowded. Tee's business is doing well, and Q is proud of her. She has come up through the ranks in the salon business. Now, she is one of the front runners.

Getting out of the car, Q heads inside the salon. Beep-Beep. His phone is going crazy. He reads the first of two messages. "Room 204 Hampton Inn." The second message reads "Daddy, it's Thursday again. Pick me up tomorrow. I love you Keonne." Looking at his last message, he smiles. "I love you too Lil' Mama," he says to himself. They went to Carowinds the week during Tim's accident, but Keonne would never miss seeing her daddy two weeks in a row.

"Hey Q," someone says, breaking his train of thought. It's Elbony walking out the salon.

"What up El? Where you headin'?"

"Oh, nowhere special Q, just picking up lunch for everybody."

"Aight then, lil' sis."

Tee is looking through a hair design book with a client when Q walks in. She looks up and smiles at him as he heads to the back office to call his daughter. He talks to Keonne for a few minutes, well, listens to

Keonne give him her list of things she has planned for the weekend, like any other daddy's girl, he agrees and says he will see her tomorrow.

"Early daddy!" she responds.

Q calls Dina and sits to wait for Tee to get a break from her clients. Looking at his watch, it is 10:45 a.m. He is meeting Van at 12:00 for lunch at Golden Corral. Tee walks in looking a little strange.

"What is it Tee?" Q says, not knowing what to expect.

"I'm cool Q, just tired of standing on my feet so long. We've been backed up ever since Terri's been gone. I spoke with her this morning before we opened. She promised to start putting in some hours come Monday. Whew! That is some of the best news I had in a while to start my day," she says sitting on her couch.

Q sits beside her before he speaks. "Come 'ere ma!" Grabbing her, he slowly removes her shoes. He starts to massage her feet.

"Mmmmmm!" she moans. "That feels good Boo. I see you haven't lost your touch."

"Never that," he replies. "Never that."

After relieving some of the stress Tee is feeling, Q finally leaves to meet Van for lunch. The Golden Corral is crowded for a Thursday. He spots Van sitting at one of the booths close to the back behind the salad bar. She greets him first by looking at her watch.

"Don't even try it ma, I'm on time."

"Yeah, you're on time baby, but that's what scares me. You're usually never on time!" she says, pinching his arm. They enjoy lunch together while discussing their situation.

Van speaks up first, "You know, Baby Rasta's sacrificing a lot by getting involved in this. He really thinks a lot of the whole crew."

"Yeah, you're right ma. You don't meet many people in The Game like Rasta. To us, it's only a come up. But to him, this shit is business. They live and die for this hustle game. Me and The Crew have counted out millions of dollars with Ras and his people. Never once have we come up short. That alone will gain the respect of your connect. So when we have differences, they feel it's their problem too. It's trouble enough with one mad rasta, but when you got more than one, be ready for blood."

Q sees Van home and heads to the Hampton Inn. His thoughts

return to Baby Rasta. Rasta had shown up on The Block outta the blue. After meeting him, he told Q his reason for being there.

"Rasta, I appreciate you wanting to help, but I..."

"But what, mun? Baby Rasta feels like you dissin' him mun. You're my brethren."

Q knows there is no use in arguing with Ras. "Aight Baby, what's your plan?" Q asks him.

"Listen to me, mun. Meet my sister." Rasta's sister's name is Inga AKA Poison. She is fine. Before Q can put his pimp game down, Rasta gives him the low-down on her. She is deadly, already with seven bodies to her credit. She has earned her nickname "Poison" from her ability to lure some of the most difficult targets into her wrath. Looking at her, Q paints a clear picture in his mind of the surprised look her adversaries must have had on their faces when the Black Goddess stands before them, naked with them almond eyes, nothing more than Morning Star himself... Death. Shaking the thoughts from his mind is a lot easier than shaking off the chill his body is feeling. He knew it could have been him that got caught slipping. "Damn," he says to himself, "a hard dick ain't got no fuckin' conscience. I've got to slow my black ass down!"

Chapter Sixteen

Dying With Your Boots On

Knock-Knock-Knock. Dina opens the door wrapped in only a sheet. She says, "I ordered pizza if you haven't already eaten."

"I'm cool right now ma. I ate something earlier."

Dina runs water in the Jacuzzi for Q. He lies his head back enjoying the sensations throughout his body. His mind drifts back to Rasta's sister. There is no way he would ever take a chance on becoming one of her victims.

Dina's voice causes him to open his eyes. "Do you mind if I join you?"

She no longer has the sheet wrapped around her body. Q thinks of Rasta's sister once more before his manliness takes control. "Well," he mumbles to himself, "so much for slowing down".

"Did you say something?" Dina says, now in the water with him.

"Nah ma, come 'ere'?"

TWO DAYS LATER, Q MEETS DINA OUTSIDE OF WADESBORO. IT'S time to bring the rest of the plan together. "What's up Dina?" says Q.

"Sorry I'm late ma. This is my main man, Baby Rasta. He'll be going with you."

"Hey Rasta," she says, handing him her hand.

Rasta responds, "No disrespect mun, but ya' beau-ti-ful mun. Just like the boom-ba-clot sunshine. Q, how can you keep something so beau-ti-ful waiting, mun?"

Dina loves Rasta's accent. He is only about five feet six inches tall, but Q knows the damage he can do. He is known throughout Jamaica as the "Ghost". His brother was murdered in a spot in Kingston a few years back. Baby Rasta infiltrated the spot, and by the time they knew who he was, he was already gone, leaving eleven bodies.

Q, Rasta, and Dina sit and eat lunch while discussing the situation at hand. Q tells Dina, "Dina, you just do as you would normally do on the days you and yo' girls hang on Salisbury Street."

"Aight, but I don't know how much longer I can stand seein' this nigga who murdered my brother for nothin' walk around like he some kinda God."

"Just hold on ma," says Q. "He might think his ass is God or sum'em, but when I leave The Boro the next time I stop through, Tex will make one more ride down Salisbury Street on his way to the cemetery."

TIM FINALLY COMES OUT OF HIS COMA. AS SOON AS HE CAN, HE tells Q and the rest of The Crew what went down, everybody has vengeance in their hearts. None worse than Q or June. Tension becomes thick enough to cut with a razor, but Q holds The Crew together.

Q later hangs with The Crew and can see that their money is still booming. He even stops by their other spot which is set up just like he tells them. They have more drugs pumping outta that bitch than Kerr and Walgreen put together!

"Damn nigga, y'all got this spot jumpin' huh?" says Q.

June responds, "Yeah homie, we probably do about eight to ten a week in breakdowns. The Block is mostly where the weight is sold."

"Aight homie, let's roll," says Q. "I have to meet Van in an hour."

Q gets home before Van for a change. He showers and starts cooking something to eat when Van walks in the house.

"Mmmmm, something smells good Boo," she says, walking up behind him and squeezing him softly.

"What's up ma? I didn't hear you pull up."

"That's because you have the music so loud," she says, reaching for the remote. "And why's my baby locked in the garage?" referring to Bear.

"Because he thinks he's running my house ma," Q says, turning and grabbing her gently.

"He does when you're not here mister. Now, go get my baby," she says, giving him an elbow.

"Aight ma, let me get these steaks done."

After eating, they lay in their den in front of the fireplace. Bear is snoring lightly on his rug. Van speaks up, "You know, Terri called me on my cell earlier."

"Oh yeah?" says Q.

"Yeah. She says Tim is doing well and will be starting his rehab next week." Turning serious, she continues. "Baby, it's time to put an end to all this nonsense. We almost lost another family member to these streets. That could easily have been you or me. I don't want to know how it will be handled. I trust your judgment. If you need me I'm here." Sitting up, she reaches for a box on the table. "I think you might need this," she says, pulling his Colt's twin brother from the box.

"Thanks ma," he says, taking his horse from her and getting the feel of it all over again. Q hasn't carried both his guns in over a year. There is no need since he is no longer in The Game. "I'll make sure I use this one to cut Tim's name in them niggas."

"Be careful, love."

"I will."

Q makes love to Van as if it's their last time.

Early the next morning, while getting dressed, Q is lost in his own thoughts. Van's voice snaps him out of his trance back to the present.

"Why didn't you wake me, Baby," she says. "Would you like something to eat?"

"Nah ma, I'm cool." She notices how mellow his mood has become over the past few days. Tim's condition has gotten a lot better since the shooting. But as his wounds are healing, Q's wounds are becoming deeper and deeper.

Now sitting up in the bed, she calls him over to her. "My phone lines will be open at all times. If for some reason you can't reach me, call Kiki's cell. I won't call you... It will only cause more distractions." Reaching behind her neck, she loosens the chain Q had given her years ago.

"What are you doing Boo?" he asks.

"What does it look like, Q? I'm going to war with you," she says, placing the chain around his neck. "We're ONE, remember?"

Q just stares at her, not surprised, but grateful she belongs to him. Van's status as a soldier is on a level most females can only dream of.

<hr>

Salisbury Street is busy. All the local hustlers are out getting their grind on. Most of them have four or five runners working for them.

The whole strip is only about one thing... Drugs. Da Da is supplying almost 100% of the product being sold. Sitting on the hood of his Impala, he exhales smoke from his nostrils before he speaks. "Damn Tex, this fuckin' hydro is that killa' homie! It's got me fucked up!"

"Yeah, me too. Especially chasin' it wit' this mothafuckin' Hen- dog. So what's up wit' yo' new connect Da? It must be his shit that got these heads walkin' around lookin' like this."

"Yeah Tex, we put that new shit on the strip about two days ago, and it's drivin' the fiends crazy, homie."

"Man, you have to turn me on to this nigga, Da."

"Not right now, homie. I just got plugged in myself. Maybe you'll get to meet her after I'm locked in."

"Her?!? What the fuck you mean *her* Da Da?"

"Just what I said nigga. Once I'm locked all the way in, then you can meet her."

Tex continues to sip on his Hennessey, thinking about what Da Da has just told him. A female putting this type of shit on the streets? *This nigga gots to plug me into this bitch* he thinks to himself. *Once I'm plugged in, Da Da's services will no longer be needed.*

A group of winos and some dope fiends all gather around a small barrel beside the Mini-Mart on The Strip. Whenever a fiend sees a sell coming through, they'll cut them off before another fiend has a chance to get the sell. J.R., Snake, Huck, and Jackie-D all stand around the fire talking to the new wino with the funny accent.

"Pass the bottle Lil' Man," says Jackie-D.

Snake breaks into the conversation. "I got 75 cent on another bottle," he yells.

Jackie-D responds, "Nigga, you just got ten dollars from that nigga Tex."

Hearing his name makes the one called Lil' Man become alert, hiding under his ragged coat and beat up hat.

"Yeah, he just gave me $10, but we just finished smokin' that shit up nigga. He wants us to meet him at the car wash at 9:00 tomorrow morning to clean both his cars."

Jackie responds. "Shit nigga, we'll be there at eight. That's at least forty, fifty dollars."

"Yeah, but you know Tex never gets there before 9:30." Jackie breaks toward the side of the store, cutting off a potential sale.

Lil' Man looks to Snake. "I got two bucks, mun. Pu' tit on the bottle."

Snake reaches for the two wrinkled up bills. Lil' Man snatches them back. "What the fuck you doing?" Snake says, his hand now trembling from his need of the fresh bottle.

"Take me tomorrow. I need to make hustle too, mun."

"Aight, you can roll. Now give me those two bucks before the store closes."

"Yeah mun, stop that blood-clot cryin'."

After all the other winos have passed out from wine and everything else they could destroy their brains with, the one called Lil' Man eases away from the fire. Cutting silently between houses, he finds his way to the next street over. He scopes out the scene before walking out in plain view. Sitting farther down the street off the main road, a car flashes its headlights on and off. Seeing his signal, Lil Man steps out and begins to walk toward the car. When he reaches it, he jumps in the passenger side before it slowly creeps off. The driver talks first. "Are you aight, brotha'?"

"Everything is aight mun. Have you spoken to Q?"

"Ah yes mun, I have. He's waiting for us now."

"Take me to him," Lil' Man says.

They meet Q at Dina's apartment. When Inga enters the room first, Q catches that same funny feeling he had in his stomach when he first met her. Her presence alone is unmistakable. When Lil Man enters behind her, Q almost doesn't recognize him.

Q speaks first, "Baby Ras, what the fuck did you do homie? What happened to yo' dreads?"

"Couldn't do the job wit' the dreads mun. Too many people recognize the dreads."

"But you've been growin' those for twenty-five years, Ras!"

"Yeah mun, but anything for you mun."

Inga speaks without an accent. "My brother's loyalty is shown to very few. When someone gains his respect, like you have, back in our country you would be treated like a king. You talking about a man who shares his wealth with all the poor back home who can't feed themselves. Cutting his hair is just another way of saying 'Respect'. Back home our 'locks' are sacred. Honor Rasta's friendship, Q, because he honors yours."

Baby Rasta then gives everybody the low-down on Tex's moves.

Within days, he has peeped him and Da Da's daily routines.

Da Da's new connect is still blessing him with good prices. The product is so good, he couldn't keep it. He pages his connect when he is down to his last two joints.

"Yo' Da, pick up ya' cell nigga. That's probably Yuma calling back," Tex hollers at Da Da.

"Who's callin'?" Da Da says into the phone. "Did someone page Yuma?"

"Yeah Yuma, it's Da Da. What's good?"

"What's good wit' you?"

"Nothin' much, just tryin' to pick up those two sets of rims and tires."

Yuma calls her people after setting everything up. She stresses to Da

Da to make sure he is alone or there will be no transaction. He quickly agrees without thinking. Tex puts up one hell of a fight when Da Da says he is going alone. He puts the press game on Da Da about meeting his new connect. Da Da, on the other hand, knows what Tex's intentions are. Day by day, Tex becomes more and more of an enemy instead of a friend. Da Da drives out on Hwy. 74 south heading towards Morven, North Carolina. Somewhere along the road, he meets some of Yuma's people. Da Da's hunger for money and power overshadows his fears of danger. Greed clouds his mind, body, and soul. Now, it's taking him on his last ride.

After spotting Yuma's car, which is driven by one of her workers, Da Da follows it until they turn onto a long dirt road. Da Da has been in this area several times, getting his trick on, but he has never been all the way down the dirt road. At the end, it spreads out into a large open space with only nature's fence, trees, wrapped around it..

Following the car around the back of the-split level home, they pull in front of what looks to be a guest house. Da Da mumbles to himself while sitting in his car. "This bitch gettin' that paper. I wonder who else she is supplying. With the prices she throwin' off, she definitely doin' some takeover shit!"

The door opens on Yuma's car and to Da Da's surprise, a female steps out. She waves for him to follow her inside. Exiting the car, Da Da grabs his "Nina" and sticks it down his waistband. Once inside, the young lady offers him a seat and a drink. He accepts, slowly sipping his rum and coke waiting on Yuma. After about five minutes, Yuma appears in the room.

"What's up Da Da? Are you comfortable?"

"I'm aight Yuma," he says, not able to notice his own slurred speech.

After about ten more minutes, Da Da begins to feel the ill effects of the drink. He can't figure out what has taken complete control of his body. Everything in the room still looks the same. Yuma is sitting directly across from him, her lips still moving but giving no sound. Suddenly, they stop moving. Her almond shaped eyes look to the left of him. Seeing a shadow, Da Da attempts to reach for his "Nina" to no avail. He can't move. Never has his girlfriend let him down. Finally, he gives in to the struggle of trying to free himself. The shadow becomes larger. Da Da sits, watching Yuma. Her eyes now focus on him but says nothing.

Suddenly, the shadow comes to life. Only then, did Da Da's fears overwhelm him. Q stands in front of him, now hiding Yuma. Both of his hands hold chrome 45s. Flashes of his best friends Umar and Tim appear in Q's mind as he slowly raises both arms until the infrared lights on each gun join together on Da Da's forehead. Screaming, now only to be heard by himself, he looks in Q's eyes one last time. They show no anger, no hate, and no mercy. Boom... Boom... Boom... Both horses kick at the same time. Only then, out of anger, Q pumps six more into Da Da's chest, putting his lights out forever.

Chapter Seventeen

Greed

It has been two days since Tex has spoken to Da Da. The last time they talked, it was a heated discussion about him meeting Da Da's people. He knows nothing of the connect. Only that it is supposed to be a woman, but that didn't necessarily have to be true. Da Da could have been just fucking with him. He pages Ham to see if Da Da has been through.

"Ham, what up nigga? You seen my peoples?"

"Nah Tex, I haven't seen Da Da since he dropped that work off. I have been paging him all morning with our code. That nigga still hasn't hit me yet."

Tex sits there holding his cell phone thinking to himself. *Da Da never fucked around when it came to that paper. He always checked the strip at least two, three times a day.*

"Are you still there, Tex?" Ham says, still on the phone.

"Yeah homie, I'm still here. Look, Imma swing through and scoop up that cheese. You aight? Do I need to bring any clothes for the trip?"

"Yeah, homie. We might stay overnight," Ham says, speaking back to Tex in codes.

"So, bring one change of clothes, aight?"

"Aight, I'm out."

Hanging up, Tex leans his head back on the headrest of his LS 400 Lexus. "Where the fuck that nigga at?" He mumbles to himself. He knows where most of their product is kept, but since Da Da has this new connect, he knows Da Da is stashing plenty of kilo's somewhere else. He has been paying twenty-two a piece with the old connect, so Tex knows whoever this bitch is, she's caked up. *I'll just have to wait until this nigga decides to show up.*

Chapter Eighteen

Welcome Home

Back in Rockingham, on The Block, the whole crew sits in the parking lot just like old times. Everyone is there except Tim, and Q is on the way. Q has been to see Tim at the hospital a few times. Terri has been going back and forth between the hospital and the salon to be by his side.

Pulling into the parking lot, Q feels good seeing his homies together. Stepping out of the car, they all greet him.

June speaks up in front of The Crew, "What tha' deal nigga, you forgot about yo' peoples or sum 'em?"

"Never that homie, we family," Q says, giving everybody some dap. The Crew is surprised when Q tells them the news of Tim coming home in a couple of weeks.

"Damn,' says Big Kev, "He'll make it in time for our outside jam and bike rally at the club."

"Yeah Kev, he misses the whole crew."

"We should make the whole joint a coming home party for T," says Corey.

"Yeah you're right," says Fat Dave. "That nigga love that Anthony Hamilton cat."

Corey and Poo have been advertising the outside jam all over the radio stations. Just on the strength of The Crew, there will be at least twenty-five hundred bikes there. Anthony Hamilton is topping the charts with his number one hit song 'Coming Where I'm From'. Corey and Poo have been trying to get a show done through their contacts up top. His producer has called their people, letting them know he will be touring through the Carolina's, so they booked him.

"That's if we can get that nigga away from Terri long enough," says Q. "She got our homie's nose wide tha' fuck open."

"Yeah," says Big Kev. "Terri is the type of chick all of us need in our corner... a soldier."

Q hasn't seen Tee in almost two weeks. They have spoken by phone a couple times. Leaving The Block, he heads to the salon. Finally after getting a parking space, Q enters the salon. It is crowded.

"Damn," he says to himself. "If all these people are here for a hair-do, then I am in the wrong business."

Walking through the lobby, he speaks to everybody and keeps going. When he walks in where the work is going on, he finds all three chairs full. Tee, Terri, and El are all putting in work.

"What's up everybody?" he says over the loud dryers.

"Hey stranger," yells Elbony who is the closest to him. Tee already has her arms spread wide waiting on her hug.

"Mmmmmm, I missed you boy," she says, squeezing him tightly.

"I missed you too ma," he says, squeezing her just as tight.

"Save some for me?" someone yells running up, grabbing them both. It's Terri.

"What up lil' sis?" Q says while they both make a sandwich out of him.

"Nothing big bro'. Still trying to get caught up with my clients."

"That's good sis, handle yo' business."

Turning to Tee, he says to her, "What's up wit' you baby girl? I came by to scoop you up, but I see you're busy huh?"

"I'm not that busy," she lies while eyeing Terri and Elbony.

"Go 'head Tee, I'll finish Tracy up. It's only a perm," says Elbony.

"Thanks El," Tee says, grabbing her purse. "I'll be back shortly."

"Take your time gurl. We got your back," Terri yells.

"Aight y'all, I'm out. "

Q says goodbye to everybody, and they leave the salon. "So where to ma?" he says to Tee.

"My place," she says sarcastically.

"Ah, come on ma? I'm starving."

"Me too," she says, reaching behind him and gently massaging his neck. "How about Pizza Hut?"

"That's cool wit' me," he says, now feeling intoxicated from her touch. They talk about a lot of different things while they enjoy lunch.

She asks, "You know Terri's madly in love, don't you?"

"Yeah. But she's not the only one in love. Tim is the last person I ever thought would slow down."

"Maybe the shooting changed his outlook on life. Some people have to go through certain things before reality sets in. Sometimes those trials are life threatening, causing them to stop taking things for granted. I don't know exactly how Tim feels because I haven't been around him much since the shooting, but I see Terri every day, Q. She loves that boy so much it ain't funny. If something is to happen to him, or if he is taken away from her for some reason, she wouldn't live. It seems to me like Tim is that missing link in her life. Nothing matters to her right now except Lil' Ty and Tim's safety."

"Well, he'll be coming home soon ma," Q tells her.

"For real?" says Tee.

"Yeah, ma. The doctors are planning on releasing him in a couple weeks. He'll still have to continue his therapy three times a week."

"What are you two gonna do for your birthdays?" asks Tee.

"His birthday is before mine, ma."

She interrupts him. "They're only two days apart, Q!"

"Well, The Crew is thinking about having his party on the day of the bike rally."

"That would be nice, Q. I'm sure everyone misses him. Someone is getting old," she says, fiddling with the last piece of pizza.

"Nah, ma. I'm still twenty four right now!" He laughs. After spending nearly three hours together, Q drops Tee back off at the salon. Looking over in the passenger seat at her, Q can see her meek expression telling him she isn't ready for him to leave. He breaks her silence. "Baby, you think that maybe I could come over a little later?"

She smiles giving him her answer. "My bed is always home to you, Q."

"I didn't say bed, ma."

"But I did," she says, cutting him off. After kissing him on the cheek, she climbs out of the car.

"See you tonight."

"Aight, Shawty."

Picking up his cell phone, Q dials a number.

"Hello."

"Hello, may I speak to Keonne?"

"Daddy, Daddy, hey Daddy, you coming to get me?"

"Wait, slow down lil' lady. I haven't heard my favorite words yet."

"I love you, Daddy."

"I love you too lil' mama."

After talking to Keonne and her mother, Q heads for his kennel. As he is driving, his mind begins to drift back to Da Da. Just thinking about that hoe ass nigga makes heat waves rise in front of his face. Killing him is easy. Da Da shows no remorse, so why should he? Yuma, his sister, offers to dispose of the body, but Q has something different in mind. Thinking of Yuma, he keeps coming to the same conclusion... Killer. Whatever or whoever had crossed her in the past created a monster. Her most deadly weapon is her beauty. She watches in silence as Q raises his pistols shooting Da Da. But before death could set in, she slowly walks past Q's still outstretched arms and straddles Da Da's twitching body. Pulling his blood soaked head up to hers, she tongue kisses him. Q has only heard of the kiss of death before. Now, he has witnessed it. By the time Baby Rasta arrives, Da Da is already dead.

Pulling into his kennel, he sees a lot of commotion coming from the side of the yard where Skull is kept. All the other dogs were going crazy. Q jumps out of his car, running towards his storage building. One of his dogs breaks loose and runs into Skull. Finally, after opening the lock, Q grabs two break-sticks and a leash then runs in the direction of the fight. When he reaches Skull's chain space, he finds his best forty-one pound male, Tyson, going toe to toe with Skull. Tyson is smaller than Skull, but he is all bulldog. Q had rolled them against each other as young dogs. They have been arch rivals ever since. No matter how far he separates them in the kennel yard, whichever one gets loose, they find the other one.

"Damn," he says to himself. "Tyson, how tha fuck did you get off yo' chain?"

Breaking up two pitbulls is hard enough with two people, but by yourself is damn near impossible unless you are experienced doing it. Skull is still on his chain, which is good for Q but bad for him. It's too easy for a dog to get tangled in his chain causing him to break a leg. Q looks at both dogs as they fight for the best hold. After further examining them, he can tell they have only been fighting for a few minutes. There is no use in trying to break them now, especially by himself. Both dogs are still fresh. Q grabs a bucket of water and sits down to watch two of his best bulldogs try their best to please him by killing one another.

After an hour and fifteen minutes, Q picks his leash up and walks over to the two dogs. Both of them are sweating heavily. He hooks the leash to Tyson's collar then pulls one of the break-sticks from his pocket. They both sense the break-up of the fight and begin biting each other hard again. Q then pulls both Tyson and Skull to the end of Skull's chain. He holds them there while sticking the break-stick in Tyson's mouth. Skull doesn't want to let go, but he only has an ear hold. Releasing his hold, Q snatches Tyson back out of reach. Both dogs scream, wanting to go back. A tired Q smiles to himself, knowing that's what every serious bulldog owner loves to hear coming from his two warriors. No amount of pussy or money can replace that feeling.

Once the two dogs are treated for their wounds, Q feeds the rest of them and heads home. When he gets home, he messes around in the garage until he sees Van pull in the driveway. Bear jumps around, happy to see Van as well. She still has her nursing outfit on.

"Hey, Baby," she says, getting out of the car.

Q grabs her and picks her up.

"Hmmmm, that feels good," they both say.

Closing the door with his feet, he carries her inside the house. Bear growls, showing jealousy.

"Shut up Bear, we've had plenty of time together," says Van. Q takes Van straight to the shower.

"Baby, I missed you," she says, now breathing heavily as he undresses her. He takes his time bathing her body. She is sensitive to his every touch. After drying her off, he rubs on his favorite body lotion, watermelon/raspberry. Van is exhausted. He massages her until she is snoring lightly. He then showers and climbs back in bed beside her for some much needed R & R.

A knock at the door wakes them from their deep sleep. Q reaches for one of his Colts off the nightstand. Leaving the bedroom, he notices Bear is nowhere to be found. The floodlights outside are on. Reaching the door, Q doesn't use the peep-hole. Instead, he steps to the side, points the infrared at the center of the door, and calmly says, "Who dat'?"

"It's me Q," a familiar voice yells on the other side of the door.

"And hurry up, before this damn dog licks me to death!"

It's Kiki. Opening the door, Q laughs as Bear has Kiki pinned in one corner, licking her face.

"Get this damn dog, Q."

"Aight baby sis."

After moving Bear, Q gets his first look at Kiki's stomach. "Damn Kiki, what the hell is that," he asks pointing.

"It's your Godson, Q, and I'll be glad when he gets here. He's about to kick me to death. Where's Van?"

"In the bedroom asleep, ma."

"Well let her know I made it here," Kiki says as she wobbles towards the kitchen.

Van interrupts them, "Who can sleep with all this noise gurl?"

She turned to Q and hands him the phone. "It's June," she says, while following Kiki into the kitchen.

"What up my nigga?" Q says into the phone.

"What's up Q? Baby's here homie. He says it's important that he talks to you."

"Aight homie, I'm on the way."

"Yo' Van. I'll be back as soon as I can, ma."

"You need to. We've got some unfinished business, Baby!"

"Aight, sexy. I can hardly wait!"

Chapter Nineteen

The Setup

Baby Rasta is waiting on The Block for Q. They sit in the Chill-Grill and talk.

"You know they found the body today mun," says Rasta. "The po-po got that Strip on fire mun. People scared to death, Q."

"Did Inga put the body where she was told?"

"Yeah mun, Inga do as she told, mun."

Word spreads quickly about Da Da's death. Baby Rasta only tells what he knows. All over the news, the only thing that is being said is that they found a body in the dumpster without its head. Q starts to think it isn't Da Da, until they match his tattoos. *But what happened to his head?* he wonders. Then it hits him. Yuma. Had she cut Da Da's head off? From the way she had stuck her tongue in his mouth, giving him the kiss of death, Q feels she is capable of anything. He contemplates asking Rasta but quickly changes his mind.

Baby Rasta tells Q about all of Tex's hangouts. He has a complete layout of his daily routine.

"Ras', you and your sister have done more than enough. Me and The Crew can handle it from here."

"No, mun. We family. You have problem, mun, we have problem. It's respect, mun."

"Yeah Rasta, much respect."

Q is able to convince Baby Rasta to promise him that he and his sister would step to the side when it came time to settle up with Tex. He had promised Tex a killing if they ever crossed paths again, even if it meant dying in the process.

———

TEX CALLS A MEETING WITH ALL OF HIS AND DA DA'S WORKERS. Most of the younger runners are shook. One of the young hustlers speaks, "Tex, whoever did this is one vicious mothafucka homie. They cut Da Da's head off."

Tex responds, "Yeah, Lil' Bushwick, they fucked our homie up. Caught him slippin'. Da Da is a walking street Bible. Whoever set him up is close to him."

The whole group of hustlers begin staring at each other. "Wait a minute niggas. I know it isn't any of y'all. If it was, you'd already be dead. I didn't call this meeting to point fingers. Somebody knows something. If not us, then who? That's what we've got to find out. First, we pay our respect to our homie, then it's back on the grind."

"Has anyone gotten a look at our new connect's face?"

"I didn't get a good look, but it is a female." This is spoken by Ham.

"Do you remember what she's drivin'?" Tex asks.

"Yeah homie, it's dark, but I'll remember the car if I see it."

"Good. Everybody listen up."

He gives a description of the car then informs everybody to be on the lookout. They are to page him immediately and keep track of where she goes.

After hitting everybody off with their work, Tex and Ham sit alone across the street from the Mini-Mart.

"Da Da is good peoples, Tex. From the looks of it, he never had a chance," says Ham.

"That nigga had plenty of chances, Ham. I asked Da Da time and time again to let me meet this new connect. I'm willing to bet my life that greed got the best of him."

"What if his connect had nothing to do with it, Tex? I don't see no female being that gangsta. They cut our homie's head off, Tex!"

Tex sat in silence, his mind racing.

The connect is a woman, but that doesn't mean she couldn't have had men waiting. Hell, she could have killed Da Da herself. This hustle game brings all types of shit to the table. Tex's mind lapses further into the past, now oblivious to his conversation with Ham.

His thoughts turn to Dirk. Him and Da Da had thrown Dirk's body into a dumpster behind the old bait & tackle shop outside the Boro. Coincidence is a mothafucka, but there isn't enough money in the world to make Tex feel that Da Da was thrown in the same dumpster as Dirk's by chance. Whoever killed Da Da had to know he was linked to Dirk's death. *Is it those*

P.G. niggas? he thinks to himself.

"Damn Tex, you alright homie?"

"Yea Ham, I'm cool. I am just thinking 'bout our boy."

"I feel you. Shit's fucked up."

After dropping Ham off on the strip, Tex rides to the carwash to meet his favorite group of winos. They will be waiting for him to come through for his daily clean-up.

***

INGA HASN'T DONE MUCH MOVING SINCE DA DA'S DEATH. SHE hasn't played her part as Yuma since Da Da is her only connect on The Strip. No one else knows of her, at least that's what she thinks.

Inga grew up without a mother or father. They had been killed by a local kingpin from Kingston, Jamaica. Baby Rasta is the youngest. Inga, being only fifteen herself, was forced to raise her baby brother on her own. Whatever it took to feed them, she did it. Men took advantage of her young, tender body. At age eighteen, she met E'On. He was the same kingpin who had killed her parents a few years back. They hid Inga within their village, away from E'On's henchmen, but E'On always got what he wanted. Young girls were his thing. Each time she laid on her back, her hatred for men became her only resolve. On her twenty-first birthday, Inga beheaded E'On in remembrance of her mother and father.

Looking at her watch, she realizes it would soon be time to meet Baby Rasta. Grabbing her cell phone and keys, she heads out the door.

After paging Q and Dina, she heads towards The Boro. Feeling hunger pains, she stops for a bite to eat.

Coincidentally, sitting in the restaurant at his table, Ham is enjoying his food. He glances out the window and spots the familiar looking car going through the drive-thru.

"Where have I seen that car?" he mumbles to himself.

Watching the glass slowly roll down, Ham still doesn't recognize the person behind the tinted windows. It isn't the hand reaching out the window that jolts his memory, but he does recall seeing the bracelet which bore Jamaican colors on Da Da's new connect's wrist. Ham flips open his cellphone to call Tex. The car begins to pull off from the drive-thru.

"Damn," Ham mumbles to himself.

Jumping from the table, he exits the restaurant. There is no answer from Tex's phone. His voicemail picks up. "Yo' Tex, it's Ham, homie. I'm right behind our people, playa'. Call me ASAP."

Inga already knows she is being followed. Whoever it is has no experience at all. Before she left the restaurant, she had already spotted him. Instead of calling Baby Rasta or Q, she checks her purse, and then slowly smiles to herself.

Riding behind her, Ham texts Tex. After putting in the number and code, he closes his phone. "Damn, where this bitch headed? She is the last person Da Da talked to before he disappeared," he mumbles to himself. "This bitch betta' have some answers."

Spotting an empty rest area, Inga slowly pulls in front of the sign reading 'Restrooms'. Seeing no other cars, she pulls in beside the one following her, steps out of the car and heads toward the restroom. Once inside, she removes two mini machetes from her purse.

Still with no word from Tex, Ham grabs his snub-nose. After inspecting the traffic one more time, he makes his move. *Maybe I can fuck this bitch too* he thinks to himself.

Quietly, he walks into the women's restroom. Once inside, he begins kicking the stall doors in. Suddenly, the lights go out.

"What the fu ..." is all he has a chance to get out of his mouth.

Dropping his gun, he reaches for his throat which has been cut from ear to ear. No sounds can be heard, except the holes being punched throughout his body as Inga unleashes her fury upon him.

After leaving the restroom, Inga sits in her car, staring at its entryway. Her heart is pounding, not from fear, but from excitement! The excitement of being able to claim another man's soul. Slowly, she rolls away, leaving a black cloud over the rest area forever.

Da Da's funeral is packed with the typical people you have when a street soldier falls victim to The Game. Fainting family members everywhere and baby mama's trying to fight one another, instead of grieving for the headless corpse lying in the bronze casket.

A week after the funeral, Da Da's head is found in the trunk of his car behind the rock quarry in Lilesville, NC outside Wadesboro. Da Da's mother can't go through another service, so she has his body exhumed and his head placed with the rest of him.

Chapter Twenty

Kiki

"Hurry up Q, the contractions are nine minutes apart!" yells Van.

"I'm going twenty-five miles over the speed limit now!"

"Calm her down," says Q. "You have to keep her calm."

Van continues to relax Kiki as much as she can. "Kiki, just relax and breathe like you did in class."

"Fuck the class, this shit hurts!" Kiki yells.

At the hospital, the doctors are already waiting for Kiki to arrive. Her contractions are now three minutes apart. She is in full-on labor. Van goes into the delivery room while Q waits restlessly out front.

Four hours and thirty minutes later, he walks into Kiki's room and holds his Godson for the first time. Kiki breaks down when she sees the tears rolling down Q's face. She has never seen him show emotions before.

Wrapping her arms around him, Van says, "She named him Umar Jr. Isn't that beautiful Q?"

"Yeah ma, he looks just like my nigga."

Lil Umar weighs eight pounds and four ounces. Kiki's room is almost full with blue balloons and cards from all of Kiki and Umar's family and friends. Reading all of the cards makes Q think of his own family. He never involves them in his lifestyle. After his mother and father divorced, they still remained good friends. His siblings, which consists of two sisters, are his heart. Fucking with any of them is a good way to die.

The opening of the door snaps Q back from his thoughts. The whole crew walks in Kiki's room.

"What's up everybody?" Big Kev says.

June, Corey, Fat Dave, and Pooh all had more balloons.

"Where is Lil Umar?" Fat Dave says loudly towards Kiki. Still weak, she is only able to smile.

"She's very tired," says Van. "You can see Lil' Umar through the window in the incubator room."

They all exit at one time, heading to see the new member of the family. Kiki is asleep before the door closes behind them. Rubbing her, Van suggests, "She has to get some rest Q. Lil Umar took a lot out of her."

"Yeah," Q responds. "She looks exhausted."

"I'll keep a check on her while I'm here during my work hours," Van says.

"Aight ma, call me on your break."

<hr>

BACK AT HONEY'S, TERRI IS FINISHING UP HER LAST APPOINTMENT for the day. She will be leaving for the hospital as soon as she can. Tim's rehab has been going well.

"So Terri, when will you be bringin' our lil' brother home?" Tee and Elbony ask her.

"I spoke with the doctors in charge of his rehab earlier today. They're thinking about releasing him sooner than next week."

"That's great," says Tee.

"Yeah, I can't wait," Terri responds.

"Well, I'll pick Lil' Ty up from the day care, so stay as long as you want."

"Thanks Tee, you're the best friend, oops, boss, I ever had." Everyone within ears reach bursts out in laughter.

Tee points towards the front door as if to say "You're fired, now get out!!!"

It's around 6:00 p.m. when Terri arrives at the hospital.

She stops and picks up some food for Tim. She is surprised to walk in Tim's room to find him doing push-ups.

"My, do we have plenty of energy today!" she says.

"What's up Baby-Girl? I thought you were the doctor or one of his telling ass candy stripers. They don't want me doing full workouts yet, but if I don't burn some of this energy off this room's gonna drive me crazy."

"Well, are you finished? I brought you something to eat."

"Good, I'm starving. What you got besides you, ma?"

Smiling now, she answers, "I brought your favorite, shrimp fried rice and beef ribs."

"Thanks Baby. I promise I'll make all this up to you."

"You already have Tim by staying here with me."

After eating, Tim lies on his hospital bed with Terri at his side. Ever so gently, she massages his body. It has been weeks since they have held each other. Both their bodies were thirsty. Now kissing him on his chest, Terri savors his taste.

Chapter Twenty-One

Life Goes On

Sitting in Dina's apartment, Q wonders why Inga and Rasta haven't shown up yet. Both of them are all business when it comes to everything. He isn't really worried about their safety, both are dangerous. The breaking news story interrupts his train of thought. The news station is reporting a grisly murder at a rest area outside of town. The name of the victim is not disclosed, but the cause of death appears to have been at least forty stab wounds. Whoever killed the victim showed no mercy. The last report is that the victim's head is completely severed.

"No word yet?" Dina says.

"Nah, I just hit Ras again," responds Q.

"What happened?" Dina asks, pointing at the television. The police are still taping off the scene.

"I don't know, Dina. Somebody was killed at that rest area." Q's phone goes off, changing the subject. Reading the message, he breathes a sigh of relief. "Five minutes," he says. "They'll be here in five minutes."

When Baby Rasta and Inga arrive, Q sits back and listens to Rasta talk about The Strip. He's had several opportunities to kill Tex, but his word to Q is his bond.

Q can't help but notice the calmness Inga displays. She sits in silence, listening to Baby Rasta and Q discuss the situation. Her almond eyes tell Q nothing. They are beautiful, yet cold.

Ras speaks again. "We finish the job soon, mun. So many times, mun, I want to let him meet the Real Rasta. The one they call the Ghost, mun."

"You should have killed that nigga, Ras."

"No, mun. I leave it up to you, mun. He's not good for the business. Bleed him like the blood-clot coward that he is, mun."

"Don't worry, Ras. I got some shit for his ass."

The news reporter flashes back on the screen with more information on the murder at the rest stop. Baby Rasta and Dina are both glued to the TV. Q's eyes are locked with Inga's. Only this time, her eyes speak. As if they are holding their own conversation with him, they give him the answers, which confuse him. All the news reports, all that happened at that rest area, is her work.

Damn he thinks to himself. *This fine mothafucka 'bout her business.*

Inga speaks up, "Can I have a word with you alone, Q?"

Caught off guard, he fumbles with his words before recovering. "Aah... Aah... Yeah," he says walking toward Dina's kitchen. Dina and Ras continue to watch the news.

Once in the kitchen, Inga speaks softly. "He gave me no choice."

"Who is he, and what happened?" Q asks her.

She tells Q everything that went down. He sits and listens quietly while replaying it all in his mind. Inga has endured a lot of pain throughout her young life. Q contemplates asking her what took her down the dark road her life now traveled but changes his mind.

"I think that you and Rasta should be heading back. I'm grateful for everything that y'all have done."

"Q, you know how Baby Rasta works. He will look at your gratefulness as a sign of disrespect. And so do I. It's not your fault what happened today. He got what he deserved. If it isn't him on the news tonight, Q, then who would it have been?"

She is right, he agrees. He wouldn't be talking to her now.

She continues, "Baby told me about the situation with your friend. The easiest way to cause a distraction is by using one of us. Let me take that distraction off for you as a favor."

"Aight Inga, you and Ras win again. Only if I can return the favor."

"What kinda favor?" she asks.

"Anything," he answers too quickly.

"I'll keep that in mind," she says, heading back into the living room with Ras and Dina.

HEADING BACK TO ROCKINGHAM, Q THINKS ABOUT THE conversation he had with Inga. Rasta trusts his sister with his life. She has taken care of him on her own for a long time.

The day Tim was shot, someone had yelled behind him for help. It was a woman's voice. Instinct made him react. He saw her just before the lights went out. All during his battle for his life, he kept her picture with him in the darkness. No name, only a face. A face he would never forget. Once he was able to describe her to Q, it wasn't long before he had a name to match.

It hurt Q's heart knowing he would have to kill a woman. After he had spoken to Rasta about it, Ras understood.

"Let me think about it, mun" is his last response. Now Inga, AKA Poison, offers to deal with it. Q knows he would be in debt to her for life.

Chapter Twenty-Two

Death Around the Corner

Two of Tex's main men have been found murdered. The rest of his boys are scared to death. They all feel the same way... It could be one of them next. As he lies on his bed smoking a blunt, Tex blows little rings of smoke from his mouth. "Do you want another hit of this?" he asks the female lying in bed with him.

"Nah, I'm straight." It's Dina's friend Shea. She has been seeing Tex for awhile now. At first, their relationship seemed to be good like any other. Then Tex's attitude began to change. He didn't want her hangin' with Dina and Neese on The Strip. She and Dina have been like sisters since before Bolo's death. Shea had been Bolo's girl since grade school. Everyone in The Boro knew that someday they would marry.

Tex pursued Shea every day. He hated Bolo only because Shea loved him so much. He vowed to have her, even if it meant killing to accomplish it. The night Bolo was killed, he had earlier given Shea a ring and proposed to her. After she said yes, Bolo went to the local store for some snacks to celebrate. He never returned home. He was gunned down in cold blood. Shea was devastated. The next six months of her life were lived on the brink of life and death. Tex took advantage of her vulnerability. He came around when no one else would. She had heard rumors of his reputation but none of it showed in his compassion. Before she knew it, they were in a relationship. Left alone in a cold world by the love of her life, she became angry with Bolo for leaving her by herself. She looked for closure wherever she could find it.

For months, Dina didn't know about their relationship. Only when Shea started showing up with black eyes did she become suspicious. Still, up until today, Shea denied any involvement with Tex. Dina can't understand it.

Lying in his bed now, she loses herself in her own thoughts, her own pain. *How did I get to this point in my life?* As if he is right there with her, she apologizes to Bolo the same as she has done thousands and thousands of times.

Thinking back to their many heated arguments and how everything has gone down up to this point, she remembers Tex admitting to killing Bolo. Then said if she ever left him, he would kill her too. For a long time, she was afraid. But then one day, when she was lying next to him, the last straw came when he forced her to go to his mother's house.

"Shea, I need a favor from you," says Tex.

"No, Tex, I'm not do..." SMACK! SMACK!

"Bitch! I tell you what to do, you understand?"

Sobbing, she agreed with him, fearing for her life.

Once at Tex's mother's house, he and Da Da had jumped out and raised their hoods. When Tim came out the door, he went to his car. When he stepped away from his car, she called him.

"Hi, excuse me."

Hearing her, Tim had turned and faced the woman with the unforgettable blackeye and bruises on her face. Her eyes showed fear, but from what?

"Noooo," she suddenly screamed. "LOOK OUT!"

It was too late. Tim felt the pain of the first couple of shots. After that, his body went numb. Then everything became dark.

After hitting her one more time during an argument, she turns her back to Tex, a single tear falling from her eyes. *I have to do something* she thinks to herself. *Dina is my closest friend. Not only have I betrayed her, but if Bolo was alive, he would be heartbroken.* She closes her eyes and prays to God for guidance. An hour later, Tex's cell phone goes off.

After calling the number back, he jumps out of bed and begins to get dressed.

"I'll be back, Shea, make sure you be here." He makes a gesture with his trigger finger before closing the door behind him.

Shea lies in bed, listening to the fading of Tex's music. Once out of hearing range, she jumps out of bed. Only half dressed, she heads toward the door. With nowhere to go, she is afraid. She grits her teeth and says, "No, no, no. I will not let fear control me anymore." Wiping her tears, she knows what she has to do and where she has to go.

DINA SITS IN HER LIVING ROOM WATCHING TELEVISION. SHE IS exhausted from work and school. Her phone rings. Grabbing her phone, she answers it. "Hello?"

"What's up Dina?" Q asks.

"Hi, Q! Isn't this a surprise? I was just thinking about you."

"Yeah. Well, I wish I was there, so you could make some of those thoughts reality."

"You and me both."

"Don't start Dina, I've already got one speeding ticket to pay for because of you."

"Don't worry Q, I told you I'll take care of it. Bring the ticket with you the next time you come over."

"Aight ma, I..."

Dina hears a knock at the door.

"Who the hell can that be at my door?" Dina says out loud.

Getting up off her couch, she heads towards the door.

Q stops her. "Dina!" he yells into the receiver.

"Yes, I'm still here, Q."

"Who you expectin' this time of night?"

"No one, bu..."

"Don't answer the door, Dina!"

The knock gets louder this time. "Q, what am I supposed to do?" Dina asks.

"Okay, ma, look, do you have a gun?"

"Yeah I..."

"Get it," he cuts her off. "Get it now, Dina."

Frightened, she removes the gun from her purse. "Now what?" she says, sounding a little shaky.

Q tries to calm her. "It's okay, ma, just relax and take a deep breath. Walk to the door and stand to the side before you say anything. If someone tries to turn the knob, shoot through the door. Ask no questions, ma, just start shootin'."

Once positioned by the door, Dina asks in her normal voice, "Who is it?"

No answer.

"Who is it?" she asks again.

"It's me, Dina," says a voice more shaky than her own.

"Who the hell is me?" Dina asks.

"It's...it's Shea, Dina, please open up."

Reaching for the door, Q's voice stops her once again. "Make damn sure she's alone."

"Are you by yourself Shea?" Dina questions.

"Yes. Please open the door, I'm in trouble Dina. I have nowhere else to go."

Unable to hear her once best friend crying, she opens the door. Shea slides down on her knees into a fetal position. She is half naked and weeping uncontrollably.

Dina helps her inside then puts both locks back on the door. Shea wastes no time telling her everything that is and has been going on. Q is still on the phone listening to their conversation. She holds nothing back. She tells Dina everything, even the part about Tex saying he killed Bolo. She offers to go to the police and be the witness they need in court.

"No!" says Q on the other end of the phone.

"WHAT?" Dina exclaims. "Q, she is willing to testi..."

Q interrupts her. "Dina, listen to me. That nigga killed your brother in cold blood. He killed my best friend for nuthin'. Still, that isn't enough. He shot my other man, leaving him for dead, Dina! Now, look what he did to your best friend, ma. She didn't ask for that. He just caught her at her weakest point. Now, like I said Dina, hell fuckin' no, she ain't going to tha' police. I'm a kill that coward ass nigga Dina, or die tryin'.'"

She knows Q is right. Prison is too easy for Tex. He has to die. It is the only way she and her brother can ever rest in peace. "Okay Q, we won't involve any police," says Dina.

"When should I expect Rasta?"

"Sometime tomorrow. "

"And you?" she asks.

"Early in the morning, ma. Soon as I can get away."

"I'll see you then."

"Aight ma, make sure your doors and windows are locked. Don't hesitate to call me. I'm out."

Hanging up, she turns back to Shea. She is upset with her for not coming to her before now. After Shea bathes and gets herself together, they sit in Dina's apartment and talk the rest of the night. Both have missed hanging out together and the all night phone conversations.

The next morning, Dina is up early. Shea is still sound asleep. This is probably the first good night of sleep she's had in quite a while. Still there is no word from Rasta. He never calls before he comes through, so Dina will just have to wait. At about 9:00 a.m., Q calls and says he's on the way.

Dina fixes Shea something to eat and goes to wake her when she finds her sitting on the couch with her knees pulled to her chest. She is sobbing again.

"Shea, what's the matter?" Dina asks. "Talk to me. I can't help you if you don't let me know what is wrong."

No longer able to hold back, she screams, "I killed him! I killed him, Dina! I..."

"Shea. Shea." Dina shakes her violently. "Calm down. You have to stay calm."

Shea begins to speak. "I don't know his name, Dina. All I know is that he's dead."

"Who Shea? What? Where?"

"It happened at Tex's mother's house. Tex asked me to do him a favor. When I refused, he beat the shit outta me. After that, he made me park in front of his mother's house and pretend I was having car trouble.

Tex and Da Da was on the side of the house. Da Da pointed his gun at the door while Tex pointed his gun at me. He said if I tried to leave, he would kill me."

Suddenly, it all hits Dina at once. Q kept mentioning something about a distraction causing Tim to slip. He says Tim had too much street knowledge for what happened to him, without someone else being either shot or dead. Dina just stares at Shea. She is speechless. Her thoughts turn to Tim. He is not dead. She vividly remembers Q stressing to her to keep it on the low. Still watching Shea in the dim living room, two single red dots appeared on her forehead drawing Dina's attention. Frozen and unable to move, she screams with all her inner being.

"Nooooo... Q, Nooooo!"

Hearing her screams, Shea opens her eyes as Q creeps out of the shadows of the room. He keeps both of his horses' red eyes locked on Shea's forehead. Her sobs now seem to be lodged in her throat from fear. Q's face reveals nothing but calmness. His hand, steady and unmoving.

"Q, listen to me," Dina pleads. "Shea explained everything to me. I know the promise you made to Tim and the people who hurt him. I made that same promise myself about my brother Bolo. Q, I'm begging you not to kill this woman unless you're absolutely sure she did what she did on her own."

Q can hear Dina's pleas, but his desire for revenge and his own rage is at a tug of war with each other within him. With no other way of reaching him, Dina does the most dangerous thing she has ever done in her young life. She steps in front of the red dots causing them to land on her chest. Looking in his eyes, she can't tell whether she has made a mistake or what, until both arms slowly begin dropping towards the floor. Dina exhales the breath she has been holding for what seems like eternity. Q stares at her a moment before turning and walking into her bedroom. She doesn't follow him. She sits down next to Shea, who is still in semi-shock.

"Stay here while I talk to Q," says Dina. Standing now, she continues, "The door is over there. It's your choice, Shea. I want to help you, but if you walk out that door, I will not be able to save you next time." Dina turns and walks to her bedroom leaving Shea with a choice to make, which should be easy if she wants to live.

Dina finds Q staring at himself in her bedroom mirror, showing no emotion or anything. Both colts are still in his hands. She walks within his view in the mirror. They stare at each other a long moment before Q finally speaks. "It's against all the rules to let her live, Dina. Tim damn near died Shawty, all because of that bitch"

"Wait a minute Q," Dina says, cutting him off. "Listen to me. Do you think Shea would have come here if she didn't need help? Shea has been under a lot of stress too. She doesn't know Tim is still alive. Even Tex doesn't know."

"Why did she distract my man Dina? That's all I want to know."

Dina grips his arm tightly before she answers. "He beat the shit out of her then threatened to kill her if she didn't do it. Sounds familiar, don't it?"

"Yeah, that seems to be his m.o. He fits the description of a coward perfectly." Q walks back in the front room alone. He finds Shea still on the couch. He sits down directly across from her.

"I'm sorry," she murmurs. "I didn't mean to kill him, but he beat me so..." More tears roll down from her eyes.

"He's not dead Shea."

"What?"

"I said, he is not dead."

"He can't possibly be alive. I mean they kept shooting him."

"When you say 'they', are you talking about Da Da and Tex?"
She nods.

There is a knock at the door. Dina walks from her bedroom carrying Q's pistols.

"I'll answer it," she says, handing him the twin Colts.

"Who is it?" she asks through the door.

"It's me, mun. Open ti door mun."

"I'll get it Dina," says Q. "You take her to the back." Baby Rasta walks in with his sister Inga. It's the first time she has ever greeted Q with a smile. Q speaks, "What's up Baby, Inga? I..."

Baby Rasta cuts him off, "Listen mun, we have tee move, mun. Get this over wit, mun."

"Aight Baby, let me call June and my man. They will meet us on the way." Dialing June's cell phone, Q almost forgets about Shea. Another idea pops in his head.

June answers, "What's up Q?"

"What up, June. It's time, homie."

"Just say the word big homie, I'm on the way. This court case has been stressin' me anyway. Imma give these cops some'em to really talk about."

After setting up the meeting place, Q hangs up the phone. "Baby, I have a little surprise for this nigga, aight?"

"Yo! Dina!" Q yells. Dina doesn't answer but walks out with Shea. "Do you really wanna help fix this shit, Shea?"

She nods yes.

"What are you willing to do?" Q asks.

"Anything," she responds.

Q tells Rasta what happened with Shea. He understands her fears. Tex is a dangerous mothafucka, but he also understands that in order for her to live, she will have to be in it as deep as they are.

As Inga listens to Q, her facial expression changes from a slight Inga smile to her Poison version. Q saw that version the night she killed Ham. Thinking to himself, he wonders why her attitude changes so quickly. Maybe it's because of the favor she feels she owes him. Either that, or she enjoys seeing the two wrinkles Q keeps on his forehead trying to figure her ass the fuck out.

Shea agrees to go along with Q's plan. Although scared to death, she knows she has to go through with it. Riding with Q to meet June, Shea counts her blessings. That is, until they pull in front of June's car at their meeting spot. June is standing outside of his car. When the passenger door opens, Shea is face to face with the man who has intoxicated her dreams since the day she had seen him killed.

Chapter Twenty-Three

Game Over

It's 2:00 a.m. Q sits in the darkness of the room, his breathing shallow but calm. He calls Keonne and Jay-Jay first. After giving them his love, he calls Van. A groggy Van answers the phone.

"What's up ma?"

"Hi Baby, I...

"Don't talk ma, listen. Boo, sometimes people don't realize what or how much they mean to someone. That's because they take so much for granted, not realizing the love of their life is right in front of them. No matter what the situation is, you have my back. If I am wrong, ma, you still have my back. You let me know in our own privacy that I am wrong. That says a lot about your character. If something hap. . ."

"Q?" she interrupts him. "I won't settle for nothing less than you coming home, love. Remember my words Baby - 'No Mercy'. They showed none."

"I love you, ma," he says.

"I love you more. Now clear your mind of everything, Q. Even me."

"Aight Van. One."

"One." Click.

Tex pulls in his half-circle driveway. His two bull mastiffs greet him at the door of his coupe. His outside sensor lights haven't come on yet.

"That fuckin' Bushwick always leaving my lights off," he mumbles to himself, getting out of his car and heading towards the front door. When he reaches the door, the big mastiff, Sampson, growls as Tex puts his key in its lock.

"Shut up Sampson, and go to your own house." He closes the door behind him. It isn't until he reaches for his light switch that he notices the two red dots on his chest. He freezes.

A voice speaks, "You should have listened to your dog, nigga. He was tryin' to save your life. Didn't you know a dog is man's best friend?"

Through the darkness, Tex can't make out the figure sitting on his couch, but all his years of gun-slinging had him hip to the red dots. Back in the day, the O.G.s called them the devil's eyes. One on you is bad enough, but when it is two, the devil himself has come to give you your last rite. A slight movement on Tex's left catches his attention. He hears it but doesn't turn. His own thoughts are now racing.

"Who tha fuck is this in my house? Where's Bushwick and the wino Lil' Man? They were the last ones here. Stick-up boys quickly come to mind. That's what this is, a stick-up?" Tex speaks. "Uh... Uh... Look, homie. If you need some of them thangs, I can hook you up."

The voice answers, "There is only one thing that will be taken from you tonight nigga. No amount of money or drugs will allow you to keep it. That's yo' life."

He hears more movement. This time it's coming from his right. A slight fragrance invades his nostrils. *Women's perfume* he recognizes. Tex knows his closest pistol is in the next room. He will have to get past whoever this mothafucka is sitting on his couch. He knows he is only a couple of steps from his front door. He will break for his car if he gets the chance. The figure slowly stands up as the scent of perfume becomes stronger.

"I have someone I want you to meet," says the voice.

As the lights slowly become brighter, Tex's chances of survival become dimmer. He stands face to face with his most hated rival... Q.

Q speaks, "Meet Yuma, Da Da's connect. She is the last person Ham looked at in that restroom nigga."

Tex stares at Yuma for a long moment. He suddenly realizes why neither Da Da or Ham ever made it back home. Their dicks had become their guides, handing them the keys of death. A familiar voice comes into play.

"What's going on mun? Is everything aight, mun?"

"Lil' Man," Tex mumbles to himself. "He must be causing a distraction for me."

Q turns to face the voice, seeming to take his attention off of Tex momentarily.

Now Tex thinks to himself. He has nothing to lose, so he dives for the front door then rolls to his feet expecting shots at any moment... None. He heads for his coupe. As he reaches for the door, a voice freezes him.

"Excuse me, Tex," Shea says, standing with someone wearing a hoodie.

When he reaches up and removes the hood, Tex sees something he has never seen before. A walking dead man. June kills Bushwick as soon as they enter the house. All Tex has to do is look down. He is standing in Bushwick's blood.

For the first time, he truly knows what fear feels like. He snatches his door open when the first of a series of bullets tear into his body. Tim almost melts the barrel of his Mini-14. With the barrel still smoking, June grabs Tim's arm.

"Let's roll homie, it's over." After leaving Tex's place, they head towards Dina's.

Everyone rides in silence until Tim speaks. "Good job back there, ma," referring to Shea. "I appreciate your help."

"Thanks, Tim. Thank you for not dying that day and giving me a chance to say I'm sorry."

"I forgive you, Shea."

Q listens to his homie speak to Shea. He is shocked at how mellow Tim has become since the shooting. Terri is a big part in that, he is sure.

Back at Dina's apartment, everybody sits in the front room. Q calls Dina to her bedroom.

"Will you and Shea be okay until tomorrow?" he asks her.

"I think both of our burdens were lifted tonight, Q. Seeing Tex take his last ride through The Boro will only be the beginning of our long road to recovery."

Tim and June head back to Rockingham. The rest of The Crew have been waiting in the shadows for their return. Q takes Baby Rasta and Inga to Charlotte. They will take the first flight out.

After getting their rooms, Q calls Van. She answers on the first ring.

"Yes, dear."

"Why aren't you asleep, ma?"

"I couldn't sleep, Q. I told you to clear your mind of me, but I couldn't clear my mind of you. And don't forget, I have Kiki and your Godson here with me."

"Yeah, I almost forgot about that."

"When are you coming home?" she asks.

"I'll be there tomorrow. Baby Rasta is leaving in the morning."

"Early, I hope," she whispers.

"Yes, early, but I have to go Baby."

"Aight. I love you."

"Love you, too."

Chapter Twenty-Four

Old Habits Are Hard To Break

The light knock on Q's door catches him from dozing off. Stepping to the side of the door, he calmly asks, "Who is it?"

It's Inga. Opening the door, Inga is greeted by Q holding one of his horses. A slight smile creeps across her face before she says, "You should carry them both. One might become jealous of the other and decide to let you down someday."

"I'll keep that in mind."

"May I come in?" she questions. Q steps to the side, giving her room to enter. Once inside, she continues to speak. "I hope most of you and your friends' troubles are over."

"Most?" he asks, interrupting her.

"Yes, most. You can never let yourself become too relaxed in this business, Q. Whenever there seems like there is no trouble, something is wrong." Q nods his head in agreement. "Baby and I are planning to move back to our country soon. You will always be welcome in our home."

He responds, "I appreciate that Inga. I'm grateful for everything you and Baby Ras have done. Both of y'all sacrificed a lot of time and money. I owe a lifelong debt for you both risking your lives for me and my family. I will always be only a phone call away, no matter what. If there is anything I can ever do, don't hesi..."

She cuts him off. "Q, there is one thing I would like to discuss with you."

"Aight Inga, have a seat." She sits and looks directly into his eyes. Her presence alone is so strong, Q doesn't want to hold his own eye contact with her, but his ego forces him to. Never has he been intimidated by a woman. Inga is different.

"I have to ask you, what made you so cold, ma?" Maybe he will get the answers he has confused his own mind searching for.

"There is so much about me that you don't know."

"Start from the beginning," he says, hoping he chose his words correctly.

Inga begins telling Q her whole life story, starting from her and Baby Rasta's childhood. He knows they had come from a poor country, but the things Inga tells him they went through growing up, touches his soul. From the murders of their parents to this cat E'on. She had taken care of Baby, avenged her parents' deaths, yet her soul couldn't find rest. Speechless, he gives her the only comfort he knows. He walks over and sits beside her, taking her in his arms and holding her close.

Inga lies her head on his chest, quietly listening to the rhythm of his heartbeat. She thinks to herself *Ten years. Has it been that long?* She continues to think. *It has. Ten years since she has touched a man this way. Even then, it wasn't out of love, but revenge. This is different,* she breathes in. *His touch, his smell. Everything is different.* She closes her eyes and prays he won't release her.

Q feels the churning in his stomach. This isn't supposed to be happening. Her softness and gentleness starts to take control of the situation.

"Are you okay?" he mutters.

"I'm fine," she whispers, burying her head deeper in his chest.

They stay in that position for so long, Q's arms are numb from not wanting to slide his hand down. No longer able to hold out, he gently places his hand on her lower back. He knows it's a mistake when he feels a slight tremble from her body. Slowly, Q tries to ease his hand back up to her shoulders. Her hand stops him.

"Please," she mumbles.

Q massages her lower back. He is still feeling a little uncomfortable. She raises her head, looking him in the eyes. Her warm breath invading his own.

She says, "I... I... I haven't been touched by a man since...since..."

He put his hand to her mouth, giving her a look of understanding. He understands her pain. He removes his finger from her lips, replacing it with his own. Softly, he kisses her, letting his tongue invade her mouth. Her moans are muffled by her own hunger for his taste. She begins kissing him everywhere her lips could find. The next morning Inga enters the room and Q looks up at her.

She smiles. "Good morning. Can I get you something?"

"Dang, you say that like you the maid or somethin'. I'm cool lady," he says jokingly.

Sliding out of bed, he walks toward the bathroom. Q showers and dries off. Walking back into the room, he finds his clothes laid out on the bed. He eyes Inga.

She smiles once again at him. "It's our culture to take care of our men back home."

It's Q's turn to smile.

"I'm serious," she says. "Maybe one day you will be able to visit us without it being business."

"Sounds good," he responds.

"I want to thank you for everything," she says, walking up to face him.

"I'm the one who should be thanking y'all Inga..."

She cuts him off, "Q, I have never been with a man the type of way I shared with you. I hated men. Even you, Q. Before last night the only thing a man has ever brought me is pain."

She kisses him, probing her sweet tasting tongue around his mouth. Releasing him, she says, "Men have been with me, Q. But until last night, I have never been with them."

He nods his head showing he understands. She gives him a final hug.

"I'll be waiting for you, Q, untouched, just the way you left me."

There is a knock at the door. It's Baby Rasta.

Chapter Twenty-Five

My Brother's Keeper

After Baby Rasta and Inga catch their plane, Q heads for the hospital to check on Tim and June. Tim left the hospital last night without the doctor's consent. His rehab is almost complete. The nurses who come by on their regular shift would always have to page him over the loudspeaker. He would either be outside somewhere doing push-ups, or chatting with another patient.

Hearing the door, Tim and Terri both turn. Q enters his room and finds Terri at his bedside. Looking at Terri, he can see that she has been crying.

He asks, "What's the matter lil' sis?"

Silence.

Tim nudges her shoulder then says, "Tell him ma."

"Tell me what?" Q asks suspiciously, walking towards them both.

Terri answers, "He asked me to marry him, Q." She holds out her hand to show off her diamond ring.

"Welcome to the family, ma."

Q finds out that June has headed back to Rockingham. It's back to business for him and The Crew.

"So, when are you coming home," Q asks Tim.

"Soon, homie. I'm hoping to make the bike fest, but it doesn't look good."

"Damn Tim, everybody is hoping you will be there Baby Boy."

"Yeah I know, Q. But the doctors want to run a few more tests."

They talk for a while before Q has to bounce.

"Do you think he went for it?" Tim asks Terri.

"Yea, I think so. They will be surprised to see you."

"US, ma," he corrects her. "Us."

Q rides in silence thinking and contemplating to himself. *This whole mess started over nothing. No one gained from it, but everybody lost.* He has done something that most thought impossible. He has walked away from the dope game in one piece. Can he ever walk away from his lust for women and be faithful to the love of his life, Van? Only time will tell.

AT HER JOB, VAN TRIES TO KEEP BUSY. SHE HAS ALREADY CHECKED her phone a hundred times. She has even called Kiki. Still no word from Q. She wants to call him but decides not to. "He's okay," she keeps saying to herself. "He's okay."

Van keeps herself so busy, she almost misses her lunch break. She heads towards her office to eat the lunch she brought with her. Rushing, she almost doesn't see the roses and envelope. She opens it:

> Van, Baby girl,
>
> Without you, I'm nothing. With you, I am everything that I have ever wanted to be. If God would have made you any more perfect, he would have kept you for himself. Now turn around.

She turns to find Q standing behind the door. Running to him, she jumps into his arms, wrapping herself around him. "I'm glad you're home, Baby."

"Yeah, me too ma. Home to stay."

Q hangs around the office until Van gets off work. They follow each other to Peking-Wok for Chinese food. After ordering their food, they sit and talk.

Q says, "You know Tim will be at the Bike fest."

"That will be good," she answers.

"But I thought Terri said he won't be finished with his rehab."

"She probably did, ma. They told me the same thing. But the doctor told me he will be released on the 13th. I think he wants to surprise the whole Crew."

"Well, I think you should let it be a surprise, if that's what he's planning."

"I will," he responds.

Q can feel his phone vibrating. He ignores it as long as he can. Checking his messages, he notices one of The Crews connects downtown number. After calling him back, Q hangs up and tells Van what is going on.

"The word downtown is that D.A.'s plannin' on dropping the murder charges against June. We have to make sure he stays out of trouble at least that long, ma."

She gives him a bewildered look.

He continues, "Yeah ma, I feel the same way. Let's just hope nobody crosses that nigga before then."

After eating, they head for Q's kennel. It has been a few days since Q has seen his dogs. His father keeps a check on them while he's gone. As they stand and look over the kennel, Van says. "We should move out here someday, Boo. Build our dream house out this way."

Q had purchased five acres of land, so there is plenty of room. "Someday we will, ma. Right over there," he says pointing.

From the kennel, they split up. Van heads home while Q makes a few more stops. He calls Tim's room.

Tim answers.

"Hello. What up T?"

"What's up, Q.? What's tha deal?"

"Nuthin' my nigga, is Terri still there?"

"Nah, she had to be at the salon by twelve. Had a few appointments coming through."

"I spoke with the doctor before I left homie," says Q.

"Shit," Tim says, "I forgot to tell the doctor."

"Don't worry, T, I didn't say anything to The Crew."

"Thanks Q."

"No problem, fam. I can't wait to see you back home myself."

They talk for a while longer before Q hangs up and calls the salon.

"Hello, Honey's, how can I help you?" Tee says with a brightness in her voice.

"Hey stranger," says Q.

"Hi, Baby!" she responds. "I was just talking about you, mister."

"Oh, yeah. Was it good or bad, ma?"

"It's bad," somebody yells in the background.

"Never that," Tee whispers into the phone.

They talk for a while about the salon. When Q closes his flip-phone, he is sitting on East Washington Street. He sits in his car, scoping out the scene. Looking at the fiends walking around all zombie-like makes him dislike The Game even more. He can only hope that the rest of The Crew will one day see what he sees and leave The Game for good. Q's attention is drawn to a black sedan sitting in Nelson's Funeral Home parking lot, camouflaging itself between the rest of the black cars. He is positive they are snapping pictures.

From where Q sits, it's a clear view of the whole block. None of The Crew will be seen outside, but Q knows they are there. Opening his phone, he calls June's cell. Like he figures, June, Fat Dave, and Corey, are all in Janie's getting their eat on. After giving them the lowdown on the car parked at the funeral home, all three exit through the back. They inform all the small-time hustlers and runners on the Po-Po. Quickly, The Block is a ghost town. An hour or so later, the black sedan slowly pulls out of the parking lot and leaves. Q sits in silence, thinking to himself. *Why hadn't one of The Crew's contacts downtown put them up on what he just witnessed?*

They all decide to meet at The Club. Big Kev and Poo are already there. The Bike Fest is only two days away. The outside stage has already been set up.

"Who do you think those cats were, Q?" June asks.

"I don't know, homie. I talked to our people downtown on the way here and they know nothin' about them. I think everybody should stay off The Block until we find out somethin'."

They all agree with Q and decide not to do any type of business on the set until their connect tells them something.

Chapter Twenty-Six

Wipe The Tears From Your Lonely Eyes

Tex's body has been identified and claimed within days. His body now lies in Smith's Funeral Home. The wait is almost over. Lonely sobs can be heard throughout the building. Tex has terrorized The Boro for years. Most people around The Boro still don't believe the notorious "Gun For Hire" is really dead. However, they keep their fingers crossed, hoping the rumors are true that he is.

Raising to her feet, Tex's mother gently makes the sign of the cross over her chest. One last look at the closed casket, she mumbles the words, "I love you baby." There are very few things in life that are unbreakable. No matter the circumstances, nothing breaks the bond of a mother's love. Mrs. Johnson turns and walks out of the empty funeral home, leaving her only son.

Dina and Shea are slowly becoming close friends again. But today is a day that neither would ever forget. This is the day they lost a brother and a boyfriend. Every year, they visit him on this day. For the past two years, they went at separate times. Leaving the flower shop, they head to Wadesboro Memorial Cemetery. Before they arrive, both are in tears. As they reach Bolo's grave site, the sobbing continues.

Dina and Shea are so caught up in their grief, they don't notice the freshly dug grave only two plots down from Bolo's.

They pay their respects and are getting ready to leave when they notice the black hearse entering the double gated entrance of the cemetery. Only one car follows with its headlights on. They stand motionless as the hearse stops almost directly in front of them. As they walk towards their car, the door on the single car opens. It's Tex's mother. After a long stare, she speaks. "I'm sorry about your brother, young lady. He was a good boy."

Dina nods her head, making one lonely tear fall from her eyes. Unsure what to say to the woman who had produced the killer of her brother, she thinks her silence will be the best response. Shea, recognizing that both women are uncomfortable, grabs Dina and motions her off.

Chapter Twenty-Seven

Can't Trust No One

Officer Jacobs has eight years in as a deputy sheriff. He has gone from being a behind the desk petty officer to second in charge over the narcotics department. His partner and senior officer goes by the name of Stokely. Jacobs is a good cop, receiving several awards and bonuses for his outstanding work in the community. He is mainly noted for bringing down some of the biggest drug operations in Rockingham and surrounding counties.

Having access to the evidence room and anything else dealing with narcotics had one day gotten the best of him. "No one will miss it," he kept saying to himself. Eventually, Jacobs went from snorting less than a quarter gram of cocaine every two days to close to a quarter ounce a day. At first, he would cover his tracks by going around the neighborhood to different known drug areas busting petty drug dealers, taking their money and all the drugs confiscated from them or whatever was thrown on the ground. Since crack had hit so hard in the 90's, Jacobs hardly ever ran into a drug bust involving powdered cocaine. He had to find another way to support his habit.

The Block is known throughout the police department as the "Red Zone." Its location has been circled on the board. Officer Jacobs has patrolled The Block several times while on duty. Whenever he saw one of The Crew members, he would search them. On a few occasions, he found weapons. In exchange for not going downtown, he would take payoffs. From there, it went to giving information, then hauling kilos.

Unknown to him is the fact that his partner is also on The Crew's payroll. That is until the department brought in the S-R-T (Special Response Team). They are brought in to clean up the heavy drug activity in the neighborhoods. After making several arrests, they began hearing cases. During different trials, evidence either came up missing or had been tampered with. After an internal investigation, Officer Stokely is approached by the SBI (State Bureau of Investigation) about his partner.

Seeing a chance to cover his own tracks, he agrees to help them with a sting operation, beginning with his partner. The next few weeks, they gather all the information they can on Jacobs. The final straw comes when they plant three kilos of powdered cocaine in the evidence room with a built-in transmitter. Within forty-eight hours, it's taken. Using a tracking device, they locate the drugs at Jacobs' residence. Guilty. Instead of being arrested, he agrees to help gather enough evidence on the P.G. Crew for an indictment.

Q hasn't been involved in the drug game in almost two years now, but he still relies on his street instincts. Street instincts which have been telling him the last few weeks something isn't right. He tells the rest of The Crew to stay out of sight as much as possible and absolutely no drug transactions out in the open.

Since the Bike Fest, Tee hasn't spoken much with Q . Seeing Q enjoying himself with Van so much dulls her spirits. She left without telling anyone, including Elbony. Even though Q had wife Van up, Tee still feels like one day they will be together. Especially with the secret she is now keeping.

Now sitting in her lobby area after closing, her thoughts of Q are interrupted by the black car sitting across the street. The same car she has seen for the past three days. "Why would someone be watching the shop?" she mumbles to herself. Robbery crosses her mind. Maybe they are waiting for her to leave. She quickly shakes away that thought. If they are planning any type of stick-up, they wouldn't give themselves away like that. Grabbing her purse, she removes her .38. Then, she opens her cell and dials June's number, not wanting to confuse Q or herself anymore than she already has. Within minutes, June is on the phone.

"I'm on the way sis, don't move." When June pulls up, Tee unlocks the entrance way door, stepping outside to meet him.

"What's going on sis?"

"I don't know," she responds. "There is someone watching my shop from across the street," she says pointing in the direction she had last seen the sedan.

Before June can respond, Q is pulling in the salon's parking lot. Tee gives June a look as if asking him "why didn't you tell me you called him."

June senses it and says, "I... I forgot to tell you I called Q."

"Damn, June! If I had wanted him to know, I would have called him myself!"

"I'm sorry sis, but either way, someone is going to be mad at me."

Q steps out of the car with a concerned look on his face. He still doesn't speak to Tee as June explains what is going on. Afterwards, Q turns to Tee.

"Are you okay, Tee?"

"I'm fine," she says.

Q's voice is low and serious as he continues. "Is it a black car?"

She nods.

"When was the first time you noticed the car there, Tee?"

"Three days ago."

"Three days?" Q asks as if not believing what he just heard.

"About three days ago, Q," Tee says again with a heavy sigh.

"Why didn't you call me, Tee?"

"Why didn't I? Because you were too damn busy! You always too busy for me. Damn Q, just go home and take care of Van. That's where you decided to be. Just go!" she demands, before walking back into the salon.

Q doesn't follow her, but he does talk a few more minutes with June.

Q looks at June with a confused look and says, "Homie, our connects downtown are either slippin', or they know what's going on."

"Maybe they're involved," June suggests.

"Yeah, I was thinking the same thing. You have to stay out of the way, homie. Your case is supposed to be dismissed this time up in court."

"Yeah, but why would someone be taking pictures of Tee's salon?"

"I don't know fam, but I intend to find out."

After June leaves to inform the rest of The Crew, Q steps into the salon with Tee. He finds her in her office sitting on her recliner. For a long moment, they stare at one another without speaking. Finally, Q breaks the ice.

"Tee, listen to me, ma. We have our differences, I'll be the first to admit that. But whoever that is out there today could have been anybody. You know I love you, ma, and I know I hurt you, but that's no excuse for not calling. If those mothafuckas were stick-up boys, you would be dead by now Tee."

She knows Q is heated. He hardly ever curses during their personal conversations.

"Promise me, ma. Promise me right now that it won't happen again."

She doesn't respond. She knows Q is right, anything could have happened. Q grabs Tee by her waist and pulls her close

"What's been going on with you lately?"

"You haven't been returning my calls or anything"

Tee wants to desperately tell him what has been on her mind. But she doesn't know how to tell him that she is carrying his child since him and Van seem to be so happy together. Tee doesn't know if he would want her to keep the child or do the unthinkable. So, she is buying time until she can figure out a way to drop the news on him.

"It's nothing, Q, nothing"

As he sits staring at her, he knows that he still has love for Tee. *Damn, why can't I have both?* he asks himself. Before leaving the salon, Q promises that he will stop by her condo later.

TIM IS FLIPPING THROUGH THE CHANNELS WHEN TERRI WALKS through the door. "What up ma," he says.

"Hi Baby," Terri responds. "Where's lil' man?"

"He's asleep, ma."

Terri walks over to the couch beside him, sitting down and kicking her shoes off. "My feet are killing me," she says.

"Let me take care of them for you, Boo." Tim grabs both feet giving her a long gentle massage. After carrying her to the bedroom, he makes love to Terri until their bodies collapse. Now they lie in each other's arms enjoying one another's company.

Tim says, "You know Mrs. Johnson called again today."

"Yeah, I figured she would. She called me twice at the shop."

"What do you think we should do, Baby? I know she misses her grandson, but we've been through so much lately, I'm still a little uncomfortable leaving Lil' Ty with anybody."

"Mrs. Johnson is not just anybody, Terri. I was shot the day we met her, but I still remember the concern she had for her grandbaby's safety, ma. That old lady is scared to death."

"I understand that, Tim, but she could've warned us before we got there."

"No, she couldn't, Terri. Mrs. Johnson did everything she could that day to save Lil' Ty. Trust me ma, if she would have given us the slightest bit of warning..." He pauses a second then continues, "We would've found her and Lil' Ty both dead."

Terri stares at the ceiling as Tim strokes her long silky hair. "I think she has suffered enough," Terri says.

Picking up the phone, Tim doesn't say anything but nods his head, showing his approval. "Hello, Johnson's residence."

"Hello, Mrs. Johnson, this is Terri. Are you busy?" Terri can hear Mrs. Johnson's sobs seeping through the receiver.

"Don't worry Mrs. Johnson, Lil' Ty is fine, but he misses his grandmother dearly."

Through tears of joy, Mrs. Johnson speaks. "Thank you, my child. Thank you, Thank you, Thank you."

Terri makes plans to meet Lil' Ty's grandmother at the salon after work the next day. Hanging up the phone, she feels as if a heavy burden has been lifted from her.

"You're a special person with a forgiving heart," Tim tells her. "Wifey material," he mumbles to himself.

"Did you say something?" she asks.

"Nah ma, just reminding myself how lucky I am to have someone like you."

Terri blushes, lying her head on Tim's chest, giving her own thanks for having him. Closing her eyes, she drifts off into a deep sleep.

The next day, Q receives the phone call he's been looking for. Hanging up the phone, he taps Van on the shoulder. "Wake up, ma."

After waking Van, he explains what he just found out on the phone.

"What about you, Baby? You haven't done any type of business in nearly two years."

"Yeah I know ma, but you can't put anything past these people. If we can hire two of them to haul cocaine, then there is no limit to what they will do to protect their own asses." Q can see the worry in Van's eyes. "Don't worry. Anything they come wit, they're gonna have to prove it." He continues, "It's not me I'm really worried about. Everybody already knows that I'm out of The Game, but The Crew is my second family. We can only hope that the knowledge they learned is put to good use."

Q's thoughts are correct. Officer Jacobs can't get the pictures he needs for a full fledged indictment. Jacobs has checked every property Q owns, all his vehicles, everything. Unable to find any flaws, he checks his associates, beginning with one Tashonda Davis. Jacobs goes over her assets with a fine tooth comb. He himself is impressed with her CEO skills. Officer Jacobs doesn't want to pry too far into Q's immediate family's assets. He doesn't know how financially stable they are, but he knows Q never involves them in any type of illegal activity.

If news of him running background checks on any of them is somehow leaked out, Jacobs knows his family is as good as dead. For weeks, Officer Jacobs scopes out different locations The Crew members hang out at. Still nothing, no concrete evidence. Desperate now, he plots against The Crew. He thinks of ways to plant narcotics on each of them. It will be dangerous, but Jacobs is quickly running out of time.

Chapter Twenty-Eight

Keep It On The Low

The whole Crew sits in the back office of The Club. Q finishes giving them the low-down on their connects downtown. June speaks. "Yo' Q, we basically left everything the way it was when you left. We never do business out in the open, and everything we buy, it's legit."

"Good," Q replies. "That's probably the first thing they'll check."

"What about The Club?" Q asks Big Kev and Poo.

"I just got off the phone with our lawyer who did the contract," Poo answers. "We're good, Q."

"Aight, homie." Q reaches down and picks up his gym bag. Placing it on the table, he unzips it, then removes a package from inside. "Just a little insurance in case any of us should ever need it." Dumping the contents on the table, he reveals at least a hundred photos of Officer Jacobs and his senior officer and partner Stokely. There are several video and cassette tapes stacked neatly together.

"Damn Q, how did you come up wit' all this shit homie," Fat Dave asks, still not believing what he is looking at.

Q answers while looking over at the whole Crew. "From the first day we conducted any type of business with these two dirty mothafuckas, I got 'em right here," he says, pointing at the stack of evidence. "One of the first things you learn in this hustle game is to cover yo' own ass. These types of people will bring down everybody to keep from falling."

Big Kev asks, "What do we do now, Q?"

"We don't do nothin' homie. We continue to act as if we know nothin'. Keep the small time hustlers supplied as usual. If you hear from either of our connects, get at me. Don't call them or talk to them, they could be wired. We have enough evidence here to shake up the whole damn county. Oh yeah, one more thing," Q says before standing to leave. "Let me get that heat up off all y'all."

"WHAT!" everybody says at once.

"Relax, niggas," he says, digging deeper into his gym bag. One by one, he pulls out each Crew member's weapon of choice. He continues, "Better to be safe than sorry. Now give me them dirty ass pistols."

THE CREW CONTINUES TO SHOW THEIR FACES AROUND THE BLOCK and hood. They make sure no business is conducted out in the open. If the police don't already have them, then they won't. Down at the police department, the SRT knows they are in trouble if they don't act fast. The evidence they have gathered during their three month undercover sting operation is extremely weak. Nothing is hands on. Any half-ass lawyer would rip them apart in a court of law.

Out of desperation, they organize a sting operation called "Trick or Treat". On November 1st, the department conducts a county round-up. They kick in doors at 4:00 a.m., catching most of the hustlers off their square. Most of them either still have product on them or an asshole full of money. Between the Special Response Team, the local police, and the deputy sheriff's department, by 5:00 a.m., they had netted seventy-eight arrests, with twenty-two warrants unserved. The local paper's front page is full of mug shots. Half the pictures make most of them look like it wouldn't be long before they started drawing social security.

Closing the paper, Q speaks. "Damn, they tried to pick up the whole fuckin' county!"

"Yeah Q, they did," says Van. "I read it before you woke up this morning. Look like they still have a lot more warrants to serve from what the papers statin'. Do you think the guys are going to be okay?"

"Well, ma, usually during a round-up, most of the time, they will do buys using informants or come at you with a mothafucka wired up." He continues, "If greed doesn't get the best of a hustler, then usually he will slip through the cracks. I was in The Game a long time, and there has never been any type of major drug bust without at least one or two 'Big Fish' gettin' caught up with the smaller ones, trying not to miss a dolla'. All we can do is hope our family isn't one of them."

"Did you call anybody, love?"

"Nah, ma, if something happens they will know exactly what to do."

Van pulls her nightgown over her head and straddles him. Q stares at his black queen, now facing him sitting on his lap. Her aroma fills the room. Q bends down and gently sucks on her neck. Van leans her head back, making herself more available. Van's eyes are glazed over as if she is on some type of medication.

"I love you Boo," he mumbles. Her response is only a slight smile. As they lay exhausted in their own sweat, the phone startles them.

"Hello," Van says.

"Van, this is El. I hate to bother you, but I didn't have anyone else to call."

"What's wrong, El?"

"Van, it's my brother Jason. He was picked up this morning during the sting operation."

"Hold on," Van says as she wakes Q.

"What is it babe?"

"It's El on the phone, Q. She says they picked up Jason this morning."

"WHAT!' Q says, grabbing the phone.

Elbony explains to Q the only information the authorities would give her. He later finds out that Jason's right hand man, Tech, was picked up before Jason.

"Jason Wright, you have a visitor."

As Q approaches the glass in the visiting room, Jason notices Elbony, Van, and Q have come to see him. Picking up the phone, he speaks to El first. She is his heart. After talking to Van, he finally talks with Q.

"What up homie?"

"I'm good, Q."

"What type of shit they got you down here on?"

"Right now, I don't know myself, Q. They just kicked my shit in about two hours ago, but one thing is fo' sho'. I ain't sold nobody shit."

Q nods his head in agreement. Looking through the glass at Jason, he thinks to himself. Seeing Jason in the midst of his struggle makes Q even more thankful he left The Game.

"You know they picked up Tech about an hour before they hit you homie."

"Nah, I didn't find out until I got down here. Some funny shit's going on, Q. Them mothafuckin' Feds is asking me some shit only me and that nigga Tech know about."

"Did they find anything at your crib?"

"The only thing they found is my heat and some cash."

"Aight. As soon as your bond is set, El will be here to pick you up."

Q leaves the county jail thinking about what Jason has told him. He already comes to the conclusion that Tech is snitching. Jason put Tech on when he didn't have shoes to put on his feet. Now Tech is giving thanks by telling, thinking that is his get out of jail free card. But the only thing he is getting free is a Certified Death Certificate.

Old habits are sometimes hard to break. Whenever the police make a major bust throughout the counties, Q and The Crew would always leave town for a few days until it cooled down. Even though he's had been out of the game, Q still finds himself on Highway #1 heading towards Fayetteville, NC. Before he realizes, he is running for no reason. Laughing to himself, he drives on knowing that his favorite continent is at the end of his journey... Asia!

When he shows up at her apartment, she is so excited to see him. Q feels bad because he can see the sincerity in how much she missed him. Jumping in his arms, her first words were "I love you."

His only response is a tight hug. His old lifestyle had caused him to cross paths with a lot of different women. Women he now cared deeply about. Asia is only one of many who became so close to him. Q knew women all too well not to play with their feelings or emotions, but his past is causing him to have to juggle with too many hearts.

"What's been up, Baby-Girl?" Q says.

"Nothing, Baby. I just have been missing you so much. How long you gonna stay this time?"

"Well, you know June's court case is tomorrow. Hopefully they will dismiss that shit."

"That will be good," Asia responds.

"Look, I want to let you know I will be laying low for a little while. Some shit went down, and I don't want to bring no heat on you."

"What you mean, Baby? You know I can handle whatever it is."

Q knows that shit sounded good, but nobody knows how they can hold up against that time until they are tried. And he isn't gonna test Asia on his freedom.

"Yea, I know you could, Baby, but you know I'm not trying to have anything happen to you."

They talk for a little while longer before Q heads back towards home. He wants to get a feel for where Asia's mind is. He knows you are only as strong as your weakest link. He has to make sure all ends are covered.

Chapter Twenty-Nine

Death Wish

"All rise!"

Everyone stands as the judge enters the courtroom. After taking his seat, he gives instructions to both the prosecutor and the defense attorney. He says, "What does the state recommend in the murder case of Mr. Hill?"

"Your Honor," the prosecutor says. "We're requesting a continuance."

"Mrs. Cummings," the judge interrupts her. "This is the fifth continuance in this case. Still you have produced no witnesses, not one shred of evidence against this young man." He looks over at June's attorney as he continues, "Do you have anything to add Mr. Williams before I make my final decision?"

June's lawyer makes a few short remarks dealing with the charge in the case.

The judge then hands down his decision. "I recommend that the state take a voluntary dismissal on the murder charges against Mr. Hill. This court stands adjourned."

Rap. Rap. His gavel bangs in the last words. June walks out of the courthouse once again a free man. But before the ink on his dismissal papers dry, Tech has already given statements on Jason and the whole Crew.

The detectives have banged Tech's head in about Q. They want anything they can find on him. Tech's statements are enough for the agents to haul Jason into the interrogation room. After four hours of trying to get cooperation, they finally give up. His bond is set at $250,000. Elbony pages Q as soon as she gets word. Jason is released later that afternoon. He meets Q and June inside The Chill-Grill.

Jason shakes his head and says, "Yeah Q, they asked me all type of shit, homie."

"That nigga Tech sold his soul, Q," says June.

"After everything you done for this nigga, he double crosses you."

"Yeah, that's the difference between men and dogs. You can feed niggas for years, and they will turn on you like you never did one thing for them."

"But don't worry homie, we gonna take care of that nigga."

Q DECIDES THAT HE NEEDS SOME TIME TO THINK THIS SHIT OUT. He tells Van and KiKi to get dressed, so they can head to Charlotte for some shopping. He also figures he can squeeze a couple of minutes in with Kris while he is up in the city.

Back in Rockingham, things have gotten crazy. Big Kev, Poo, Corey, and Fat Dave have been snatched up off The Block. They are being held on a state charge of conspiracy. June and Tim can't move, figuring they probably have warrants on them. They sit in Tim's apartment discussing their next move. Before they can speak, there is a loud explosion before the front door comes crashing down.

"Get on the floor! Get down! Get down!"

SRT officers come in from the front and back doors. They are hauled downtown with the rest of The Crew.

They are all charged with state conspiracy charges. Detectives are working around the clock trying to build a solid case against the notorious P.G. Crew. Each member is hauled down to the interrogation room every hour on the hour. Officer Stokely sits back and lets the SRT detectives handle the situation, while Officer Jacobs hides in the confines of his office.

Big Kev and Tim sit on their bunks discussing the situations. "Damn T, those bastards throw everything at a nigga but the kitchen sink, homie!"

"Yeah, I feel you. Fuck them niggas, Kev. If they want some info, they betta' get off their asses and go get that shit."

Before Kev can respond, the cell door opens and an officer yells. "Timothy Gregory, you have a visitor."

After giving Kev a pound, Tim exits the main cell block with the officer. As he walks by the other blocks, he can hear the rest of The Crew calling his name.

"Keep walking and don't speak," the officer orders him.

"Fuck you," Tim responds.

Entering the visiting room, Tim sees Terri through the glass window. Making eye contact brings a smile to both of their faces.

Picking up the phone, Tim speaks first. "What up ma, you aight?"

A weary eyed Terri answers, "I'm doing okay, love. Just missing you."

"Yeah, I feel the same way ma, but we both have to be strong. If not, we become the hunted, and that's something we can't allow to happen. What about our son, how is he?"

"He's doing fine. I let him spend some time with his grandmother, but he really misses you."

"I miss him too. Have you gotten in touch with Q yet?"

"Me and Tee have been calling him since yesterday, and his phone just keeps going to voicemail"

"Well, keep calling him. Hopefully they haven't picked him up too."

They talk for the whole visit, which is only an hour. The Crew's attorneys are frantically trying to get them a bond, but Officer Stokley and Jacobs fight against it with everything they have. As far as they are concerned, the P.G. Crew is as good as finished.

Q's ride home seems long. For some reason, Tee has been calling him back to back. She has even started calling from Terri's phone. He figures she probably wants to cuss him out for not showing up that night after he had promised he would see her later. Sometimes, a woman just doesn't understand that shit comes up. He knows he will need some time on the phone to clear it up but with Van and KIKi in the car, now isn't the right time.

Once he arrives home, he takes Van and KiKi's shopping bags and all the clothes they bought for little Umar in the house. "Hey babe I'm going to ride down to The Block and check on The Crew. I will be home before dinner."

"Ok, I'm making your favorite tonight, so get here before Kiki eats everything up."

After getting back into his car, he picks up his cell phone and calls Tee. No answer. "Where could she be?" he mumbles to himself. Dialing again, he puts the phone to his ear.

"Hello," Tee answers on the third ring.

"What's up Shawty," says Q.

Before Q finishes his sentence, Tee is already speaking in codes. She tells him everything that has gone down over the last few days. Crossing into town, Q doesn't know what to expect. He knows he has been out of the game for over three years now, but he also knows how dirty The Game is. He isn't worried about any of The Crew snitching. He is more worried about some trigger happy rookie cop trying to make a name for himself. Reaching inside his glove compartment, he pulls out his Colt and lays it on the seat beside him. Turning off Hwy 74, he heads toward his kennel where he had told Tee to meet him.

Pulling onto his property, his dogs greet him with the familiar sounds of their powerful necks yanking against their heavy chains. Tee hasn't arrived yet, but Q isn't worried. She is schooled by one of the best, so he knows she takes no chances. She will make sure she isn't being followed before exposing her location.

After thirty minutes of waiting, Q notices Tee pulling in the make-shift driveway. She immediately gets out and explains to Q what went down in more detail.

Her scent is driving Q crazy, but he knows he has to deal with the situation at hand. They sit and discuss every possibility that could come their way. Tee is a soldier. So is Van. She listens to Q with calmness. Her expression is meek, but he knows she is listening intently. Q grabs Tee's hand and walks her over to their storage building. After unlocking it, they both step inside.

"Ma, I need you to make sure every one of The Crew's attorneys receives a copy of each of these," he says, handing over three tapes. He continues, "Let them know that there are at least twenty-five more of these tapes along with hundreds of photos. They may snatch me up for some reason, ma. If they do, you already know how to handle this whole situation. Remember Boo, if anybody strange tries to approach you, give them 380 reasons why they shouldn't have."

Tee only nods before stepping out of the storage building. Reaching her car, she turns and faces Q. She thinks maybe this would be a good time to tell him that in a couple of months, he would be a father again. But she doesn't want to put anything else on his mind. She knows he has enough going on already.

Q stays around his kennel for a couple hours before heading home. Since he has already checked his messages on his phone, he decides to clear his voicemail. Most are so old, he just quickly hits the erase button. He presses his last message which almost causes him to have a pile-up on the highway.

Message 25: "Yo' Q, this is ya' boy Tech, homie. I've been trying to reach Jason, but he isn't in town. Look homie, I got thirteen dollars and fifty cents for a half a bag of dog food. Call me ASAP."

Q closes his phone, but not before storing the message in his memory box. His mind is so clouded with rage, he can't hear the many honking horns behind him. Only when the young white lady taps on his window does he finally come to his senses. Slowly, he eases his foot off the brake with the long line of traffic impatiently following him. He rides in silence, thinking only of the things that lie ahead. Q hopes to be able to hang his pistols up for good. Now, that thought itself seems inevitable.

The game Tech is playing is for keeps. This nigga has the nerve of trying to play like him and Q have done business together. He is trying to set Q up like he is some new kid on the block. He knows Tech is going to have to be handled, but how is the problem. Tech has his own reputation as a pistoleer. Plus, he now has the law on his side.

Chapter Thirty

When Good Cops Go Bad

Back at the courthouse, things have really become hectic. Mainly for the officers and DEA agents. Everybody is scrambling for any type of evidence against each of the P.G. Crew members.

Officer Stokely sits behind his desk, fumbling with a stack of indictments on The Crew members. After reading over the first three, he slams the whole stack on the floor yelling, "Brooks! Get in my office... ASAP!"

A very thin officer with pale skin peeks in the door as if afraid to enter.

"Get in here, Brooks!" Officer Stokely yells again, this time much louder.

Petty Officer Brooks slowly enters the office on shaky legs. "Uh... uh... yes sir," he answers.

Officer Stokely gazes at Brooks in disgust. Brooks reminds him of the shell of a man he was before he became involved with his new friend... cocaine.

Cocaine had given him the only thing he lacked growing up in the predominantly black neighborhood where he was raised. It gave him something neither of his parents nor his few black friends could. It gave him heart to stand up against the bullies he had feared all through his childhood.

Stokely asks, "Brooks, has SRT looked over the charges in these indictments?"

"Yes, sir," Brooks answers.

"Bullshit!" Stokely screams. "They will never get one conviction out of this garbage. Who approved this mess?" he questions, pointing at the stack of papers on his desk.

"The prosecutor, sir."

Stokely leans back in his office chair. His eyes tightly shut. He massages both of his temples. Opening his eyes, he gives Brooks one final order. "Get Jacobs in my office, pronto."

"Yes, sir," Brooks answers before slamming the door behind him.

Officer Jacobs is about to exit the office when his phone rings. He thinks of not answering but quickly changes his mind.

"Hello," he speaks into the receiver, as if irritated.

"Mr. Jacobs, this is Mr. Wright, The Crew mem..."

"I know who you are," Jacobs says, cutting him off. "And my answer is still no. I will not allow any of that scum the chance to get back on the stre..."

"Excuse me, Jacobs," Mr. Wright says, cutting him off this time. "I have something here in my office that I think you need to see."

"Can't it wait?" Jacobs says.

"No, it cannot."

"Give me fifteen minutes," Jacobs says before slamming down the receiver. Before exiting the office, he pulls out a small bag containing the one thing that had a solution to each and every one of his problems.

Mr. Wright sits alone in his office staring at the black television screen. He has replayed the three tapes a dozen times. As his mind drifts, he becomes lost in his thoughts. He wonders how Jacobs and Stokely let things get this far. The evidence sitting before him is enough to shake up the whole county. Then, he thought of the young lady that had delivered the tapes personally.

"Mr. Wright, there is a young lady who insists on seeing you today. I informed her that you were booked until Wednesday, sir," his secretary

informs him. Mr. Wright is about to answer through his speaker when his door suddenly flings open.

The young lady enters with his secretary right on her heels. "Excuse me ma'am, but..."

"It's okay Wanda," Mr. Wright says. Turning to the young lady, he asks, "What can I help you with, Miss... uh...?"

"Call me Teshonda." Tee doesn't say another word. She simply pulls out the three tapes from her purse. Handing them to the attorney, she then breaks her silence. "This is only the beginning," she says. "There are at least fifteen more of these plus several photos. As The Crew members' lead attorney, you are obligated to inform the people in these tapes that they have forty-eight hours for each and every one of my people to be released. If not, this evidence will bypass the mayor and on its way to the federal courthouse in Charlotte. There's no need for us to exchange contact information, sir. It's either or," she says, standing to leave. "If not me, someone will be in contact with you." She turns and walks out of the office.

It had been close to an hour since the young lady had come and gone from his office, but the watermelon/raspberry lotion perfume she wore still lingers heavily within the confines of the room. Only minutes after she leaves, his phone starts to ring non-stop. With each phone call, things become more and more disturbing. In the span of only one hour, every attorney involved in the case has received three tapes. Some contain different evidence than the others. But what shocks him the most is that they all have been delivered by a woman.

His speakerphone snaps him out of his trance. It's his secretary. "Sir, Officer Jacobs has arrived. Shall I send him in?"

"Thank you, Wanda. Send him back," he answers.

Jacobs walks in with a look on his face as if to say "What the hell is so important that I should have to rush out of my office?"

Wright meets his glance with one of his own. As he looks at Jacobs, he wonders what happened. What had happened to the young man who once was so eager to uphold the law?

"Have a seat," he tells Jacobs.

"I'll stand," is Jacobs reply.

"Suit yourself," Wright answers as he hits the rewind button on the

VCR. When the tape stops, he pushes play. As the screen comes to life, Officer Jacobs' wind seems to leave his body all at once. As if too heavy to support himself, his legs give way, causing him to collapse into the chair offered to him earlier. By the time the tape finishes, Jacobs is furious. His face is flushed with anger as he speaks.

"Where the hell did you get this? Where..."

"Sit down and shut your mouth," Wright says, cutting him off, in his own sullen growl.

"Do you realize what you have done Jacobs? Do you? If not, let me explain it to you then. This is only three of the tapes floating around town. I was advised and warned of at least fifteen more. Now, I'm telling you Jacobs..." Wright is now standing towering over him. "You take this from a damn good attorney. If any one of these tapes make it to that federal building in Charlotte, you and everybody else on them can kiss your sorry asses goodbye."

Officer Jacobs speaks through clenched teeth. "I'll see to it that none of these tapes crosses the county line. Whoever the scum is that gave these tapes to you will die."

"Scum, huh," says Wright. "Jacobs, if this information leaks out they will no longer be considered scum... You will. My suggestion to you... I think you should be heading towards the magistrates office."

"What for?" Jacobs replied.

"You have only thirty-six hours to release the scum you are referring to."

After his last statement, Attorney Wright turns his chair in the direction of the window. Jacobs knows that the conversation is over.

Chapter Thirty-One

Hitting the Bricks

I t's 2:00 a.m. on a Thursday when Q and Van receive the call.

"Yeah, what up?" Q says as he answers the phone.

"What's up homie?" It's Tim.

"What's up my nigga," Q says, now wide awake.

"Nothing much homie. I am just calling to let you know that they let us out of that mothafuckin' roach motel."

"Yeah," says Q.

"Yeah," answers Tim.

"Did they release everybody? And what about the charges, homie?"

"Yeah, homie, they came and snatched everybody out the blocks. After taking us downstairs, our attorney's met us with handwritten dismissal papers."

Q talks to Tim for a while longer before hanging up. He lies down on the bed with Van, gently rubbing his chest.

"Is everything okay love?" she asks.

"Yeah ma, everything is fine. That was Tim on the phone. They just released everybody a little while ago."

"A little while ago," she says, now sitting up looking down at him. "Q it's almost three in the morning!"

"Yeah, ma, I know. That's what I was expecting them to do. Now, they won't have to answer to reporters or worry about the newspapers."

Q is correct. Stokely and Jacobs had met with the magistrate for over four hours trying to convince him to release The Crew. The judge expressed to both officers that he is firmly against dropping any of the charges without any of The Crew members appearing in court, but finally gave in after the officers assured him more charges were to come.

It has been three weeks since The Crew had been released from custody. This is the first day the guys had gotten together. Each one has spent the entire three weeks with their better halves. Now as they all sat on the hood of their cars at the local hotspot on a cool Friday afternoon, North Park Yard, Jason fills them in on his pending case.

"Yeah fellas, my lawyer can't seem to get any type of evidence outta those mothafuckas. I keep telling him to get my shit threw out, but he keeps giving me some bullshit about some C.I. willing to take the stand."

"Don't worry, homie," says June, "If the informant is who we think it is, he won't be doing no testifyin'."

Q nods his head in agreement before he says, "Jay, look homie, if you need anything let any of us know, aight."

"I'm cool right now homie. Good lookin' out," he says.

They hang around the park all afternoon. No business is discussed, but Q can see that some of The Crew members are ready to get back on the grind. As he sits and looks over his boys, his mind begins to wonder what it would take for them to realize the hustle game is all but dead. He had to figure out a way to remove his homies from the dope game. If he didn't, he knows the only other ways out would eventually consume them... the penitentiary or death.

Chapter Thirty-Two

Honey's

Tee has been at the shop all day and into the night. It is Sunday, and she hates the idea of working on the Sabbath day, but she knows she has to get her books caught up. Her and the girls are planning a hair show, which is only five weeks away. It would be the first one that they sponsored at the salon. El and Terri are so ecstatic about the whole thing, Tee allows them to handle most of the preparations.

Jacobs and Stokely have been busy combing the streets for the last few weeks trying to get a description of the woman who delivered the tapes. Their informants have given them little or no valuable information. Both officers know their normally reliable sources fear for their lives.

Jacobs on the other hand is out of control. He has been furious at the whole Crew since finding out about the tapes. Instead of looking at it as a way out, Jacobs looks at it as blackmail. Now, no longer willing to honor his already tarnished badge, he decides to take matters into his own hands. Sitting in the driver's seat of the white van, Jacobs yells to his passenger.

"Are you sure that she is alone?"

"I've been here for almost two hours," says the passenger. "No one has come by since she put the closed sign on the door."

"Good," answers Jacobs. "Let's move."

"Wait," responds the passenger. "What are you planning to do?"

"I ask the questions, "Jacobs snarls at him. "Just follow my lead, and your case is history. Besides, I just want to question the young lady," he lies.

Tee pushes the record button on her phone when the knock comes at the front door. She is leaving El and Terri a message as she always does before she leaves the shop the night before. When she reaches the front entrance, she is surprised to see Tech standing at the front door. Tee hasn't spoken to Q in almost three weeks. She has no idea what is going on.

Opening the door, she says, "Hi ,Tech. Is there something wrong?"

"Uh... Uh... No," he answers. "I just spoke with Q, and he told me to meet him here."

"Oh, okay," says Tee, noticing how nervous Tech is acting. Her sixth sense instantly clicks in, causing her to realize that she had left her gun in her purse.

"Have a seat," she says, turning towards her office. As Tee turns, she sees the shadow before the figure pushes the door open. Her next step is followed by a sharp excruciating pain to her shoulder. Tee's limp body falls to the floor with what seems like the weight of the ceiling falling on her. Only it isn't the ceiling... It's the weight of a man. Tee has only one arm available, but she fights with every ounce of life in her body, digging her nails deep in her attacker's face.

She screams his name over and over, "Tech! Why? Tech! Why?"

The only response she hears is repeated over and over. "The tapes bitch... The tapes bitch... Where are the fuckin' tapes?"

Tech stands in shock as Jacobs unleashes his fury on Tee. Someone he has known since childhood. He knows he is a dead man from the moment he entered the shop and lied to Tee.

Jacobs has completely lost his mind. He savagely beats Tee nearly unconscious with the butt of his gun. Tech grabs Jacobs's hand in mid-swing, stopping him from his brutal assault.

"Nigga, are you crazy? You gonna kill her!"

"I don't give a damn, I need those tapes!"

"Well, she don't know or she's not talking. Either way, if she's dead it doesn't help you."

"That's ok, I got something for her ass. Help me take off her jeans"

"What! Now nigga I know you crazy. I'm not helping you do no shit like that."

"You're right and wrong. I am crazy and you are going to help me. Because if you don't, You about to get locked up for assault with attempt to kill. And I bet you will be dead before you get a chance to speak or explain."

Tech begins to help Jacobs pull down Tee's pants; he had to admit even with all the blood, she still is beautiful. Jacobs climbs on top of her and begins to force himself into Tee's tight walls. She has been beaten so badly all the fight has been taken out of her. All she can do is call on Q; she remembers how he said he would always be there for her. Jacobs continues to assault Tee with no emotion, just pure physical lust. Finally, he reaches his climax.

"Damn this bitch got some good pussy," he yells to Tech.

"Man, fuck that, let's get out of here"

"We not going anywhere until you get some of this bitch too!"

"Man, I don't want any!"

"I don't give a fuck if you want none or not. I'm not having a witness, I'm having a co-defendant. Now get your ass down there and fuck her like you want it!"

Tech, unable to look Tee in the face, turns her over and enters her from behind. It takes him a minute to get his dick hard, but he has to admit Jacobs is right; Tee's walls feel so good, he can't hold it in much longer.

"I want you to nut on her, not in her!" Jacobs screams.

Tech, now feeling the pleasure, complies and shoots his load over Tee's back.

"Now let's get the hell out of here" Jacobs says as him and Tech exit the shop.

Fifteen minutes after they leave, Tee is still laying in a pool of her own blood barely clinging to life. Her whole body is numb. She is in a deep sleep, but her thoughts seem to be wide awake. She begins to see flashes of her childhood... then her prom... graduation... Now she sees the new life in her... The baby. Tee cries from inside. She knows then that she has to live. Suddenly, she begins to pray. Praying that someone finds her before it is too late.

Tee's prayers are answered. It is Sunday night and the cleaning company always arrives around 11:45 p.m. after the shop is closed. The husband and wife who own the company did most of the cleaning themselves. They find Tee as soon as they arrive for work. She is rushed to Richmond Memorial Hospital with severe face and head trauma.

Elbony receives the call first. She still hasn't seen Tee as she sits in the emergency room. Terri is with her but hasn't said a word. She is crying uncontrollably. A doctor finally emerges from the Operating Room double doors. His sullen expression tells El and Terri that the news isn't good.

"Does Miss Davis have any immediate family here at this time?"

"No... No... No...," El screams.

"No, wait a minute young lady," the doctor says, reaching for Elbonys's flinging arms. "Calm down Miss."

El continues, "She can't be de..."

"She's not dead," the doctor says, cutting her off. "Miss Davis is alive, Miss... uh... What is your name Miss?"

"Elbony sir. Just call me Elbony."

"Alright then, Elbony. Like I said, Miss Davis is alive, but she has very severe internal injuries. The baby also seems to be fine, but we have to run some further tests."

Terri and Elbony looked at each other like "did you know?" Tee has told no one about the pregnancy.

The doctor continues, "Our hospital doesn't have the necessary equipment to treat her. She has to be airlifted to Duke Hospital in Durham, North Carolina. That is why I need an immediate family member."

Before El can respond, Tee's mother rushes into the emergency room. After getting her calmed down, the doctor explains to the mother that Tee and the baby are in very serious condition. In so many words, the doctor seems to be telling them to hope for the best, but expect the worst.

As Elbony sits and comforts Tee's mother as best she can, fear suddenly grips her causing Tee's mother to look up into Elbony's face, which has lost all of its color.

"What is it, child?" she asks. "What is..."

Elbony cuts her off by jumping from her seat and grabbing her purse. She speaks as she dials the number. "I... I... I forgot to call Q."

"Oh shit," says Terri, her face now drained of its own blood, for they know that whoever is responsible for this should have just as well stuck the gun in their own mouth, then pulled the trigger.

Chapter Thirty-Three

Welcome to Hell

Van is awakened by the phone which has been ringing for what seems like eternity. Q is still snoring lightly as she picks up the receiver.

"Hello," she says.

"Van," the voice says in a whisper.

"Yes, this is Van," she says, now sitting up. "May I ask whose cal..."

"Van, it's El."

"Oh, hi El. Let me wake up Q."

"No," Elbony says into the receiver.

"What's going on Elbony?"

"Van, there has been a terrible incident. Please listen to me. No one can reach Q on this but you..."

Van sits quietly in bed as Elbony tells her what had happened to Tee. Before she finishes, Van is wiping tears while gently rubbing Q's back. Hanging up the phone, she stares at her man. A man whom she has loved since childhood, but even she didn't know what to expect from him after this. Gently she nudges his shoulder. "Ba... Ba... Baby. Wake up."

He rolls over to face her. "What time is it ma?" he asks with sleep still in his eyes.

"Do you love me, Q?" Van asks him suddenly.

"What?" Q answers back. "Why would you…"

"Q," Van says, cutting him off. "Do you love me?"

Looking at her, Q notices that something is terribly wrong. Then he remembers hearing the phone. "Yes ma, I love you. I love you more than my own life."

Van looks directly in his eyes as she speaks. "Q, there's been a terrible incident."

"With who ma?" he says, now sitting up facing her.

"It's Tee, Q. Tee was brutally attacked at the shop by someone. She is in critical condition. That was Elbony on the phone. They airlifted her to Duke Hospital in Durham."

Before Van can finish telling Q what is going on, tears well up in his eyes. Before she finishes, they are slowly rolling down both cheeks. Q's whole body is numb from rage. He slides out from the bed and quickly gets dressed.

Even with his back turned towards her, Van can hear him sobbing. After walking up behind him, she gently embraces him as she speaks. "Q, I know that you love me Boo. I've never doubted that. I also know how you feel about Tee."

Walking around and facing him, she continues. "I've never hated her Q. I think you already know that. We only had our differences because we both saw the same beautiful person I'm staring at now. I'm just as angry as you are about what happened. But I will not let you walk out that door without me. If you die, I die."

Q steps around Van and grabs his jacket, but not before sliding both guns under each arm. Turning back towards her, they both hold onto a gaze before finally Q reaches out and grabs her hand. "Come on ma," he says. "I need you."

"Wait a minute," says Van, pulling herself from his grip.

Q is about to ask her what is going on until he sees Van pushing her chrome .380 down inside the back of her jeans. He nods his head, knowing he is going to war with one of his biggest soldiers.

By now the whole Crew has been informed about what had happened to Tee. Pandora and the girls are very upset about their friend, and the entire Crew have death in their eyes. After meeting at the hospital, they all prepare to make the drive to Durham.

Pulling June and Tim to the side, Q speaks while wiping away his tears, "I know how much Tee means to the whole Crew, but I need you both to keep them under control. I have very little details on what happened, but I intend to find out. Whoever did this to Tee, homies, whoever is involved... If I have to follow them down into the depths of hell, I will. I'm gonna murder them one by one..." Finally, he breaks down crying. His boys have never seen him emotional before.

Tim reaches out and holds Q. "It's good homie, she gonna be aight. And you right, we gonna kill these niggas a hundred times."

Q and Van leave the hospital, heading towards the salon. Q wants to see Tee badly, but he knows he has to check the shop first. Maybe the police didn't find anything, but he knows Tee. If there is some way she could have left a clue or sign, she would have.

Van rides in silence until they reach the parking lot of the salon. "Are you okay?" she asks, squeezing his hand.

"Yeah ma, I'm aight," he answers.

Q sits and stares at the salon's entrance for a moment before opening his door and stepping out of the car. Van exits the passenger side along with him. When they enter the salon, Q is very cautious before he touches anything. They find no clues in the lobby or work area. When they reach the office, Q knows this is where Tee was attacked. The place is ramshackled.

As he stares at the dried blood covering the floor, tears once again form in his eyes. As Q weeps, he silently prays. "Dear Father God. I know that I haven't been the best person that I'm capable of, but I know and believe that you are the most high God, the beginning and the end, and nothing happens except through you. I ask that you stay with Tee, Father God. Keep her safe. In your own words Father, you said an eye for an eye. Those will be my rules of the game when it's time to play."

Van and Q search the office in silence, neither find anything. Q's frustration is beginning to take control of him. Now on the verge of screaming out in anger, only Van is able to stop him by touching his shoulder. He turns to face her as she points behind the overturned desk. Quickly, he pulls back the desk to remove the blinking base of the phone that Van points at. Q pushes the play button nervously. A voice speaks through the machine. It is Tee's. "El, could you or Terri stop by the supply store in the morning for our weekly order?"

Tee continued to chat on the machine a moment longer before saying goodnight to El and Terri, but not before letting them know that she would be arriving to work late the next day. The tape then went silent except some shuffling as if Tee had stood and walked away from the machine.

Q and Van both strain their ears, hoping to catch the slightest sound that seems out of place. More shuffling... Then a voice. "Someone is in the shop with Tee," Q mumbles to himself. "But who?" he wonders while still listening intently.

After a few seconds, the voices become louder. Q knows they are heading towards the office. Then there is a loud thud like sound followed by a painful scream. Q's heart seems to stop beating as he listens to the sound he knows all too well. It is the sound of a gun-butt hitting raw flesh. Tee fights back with everything she has.

"Come on Tee, baby, tell me who did this." Q thinks out loud.

Then it happens. Tee screams, "Why Tech, why..."

He looks at Van, but before he can respond another voice comes over the recording. "Where are the tapes bitch? Where are those fuckin' tapes...?"

Tapes, Q thinks to himself. Tech doesn't know about the tapes. How could he... The sound of the last voice clears the whole picture for him. "Stop Jacobs!! That's enough. You're gonna kill her. Get off her. Let's get outta here!"

Then, he hears Tee's voice again. "Q, you said you would be here for me."

There are no tears this time. Instead, the rivers flow.

Q and Van both cry until the tears refuse to come. Q blames himself for what happened. *Poor Tee*, he thinks. He should have been there. With all the shit that is going on, he didn't make sure she was protected.

He knows Tech has crossed the line a long time ago. But what he had done that night is what gets families missing. As he thinks of Jacobs, he seems to lose control of himself. Q grabs Van's hand, pulling her to her feet. Within minutes, they are sitting outside the courthouse which holds the sheriff's office. Q checks both clips before sliding the guns back in their holsters.

Q quickly exits the car, with Van mirroring his moves. Stepping around the front of the car, Van steps up to him.

She asks, "This is it huh? After all the schooling you gave me. This is how we go out love? We walk right dab in the middle of a death trap?"

She continues, "Q, you need to think before you go up those steps. My word is my bond, love, and I stand on it," she says, now pulling out her own pistol. "If you die, I die." Click- Click. "But is this the way to do it Baby? I know they have to pay for what they did, but Tee needs you, the baby will need you."

Q looks at her like she is crazy, "What baby?"

"You don't know Tee is pregnant? El and Terri told me at the hospital. Everyone figured you already knew."

Q feels like all the air has been taken out of his body.

Van stands for what seemed like an eternity looking at him until Q walks back to the car. He gets in on the passenger side and lies his head back. She has seen that look in his eyes many times before. It is the look he gets when he becomes the judge, jury, and the executioner. Getting back into the car, he has one thing on his mind... Death.

Chapter Thirty-Four

Duke Hospital

They have already completed two surgeries on Tee. Her face is completely bandaged. The internal bleeding has stopped, but she is still in bad shape. The doctors conducting the operations are pleased with her and the baby's progress.

The whole Crew is there, except for Q. Everyone sits in silence, undoubtedly still shocked about what had happened to their friend.

It's 11:00a.m. when Q and Van finally arrive at the hospital. When they enter Tee's room, they see most of The Crew scattered around in the chairs sleeping. Van stands back as Q steps to Tee's side. Once there, he turns and motions for her to come with him. They both stare at her bandaged face before Q takes one of her hands in his own.

"I'm sorry ma," he mumbles. "I didn't mean for this to happen. I hope one day you can forgive me Tee. I guess you already know that everybody is here, huh? Well ma, I'll be here if..."

"We'll be here," Van says, cutting him off before taking Tee's other hand.

Q steps away as Van says, "You know Tee, I, ah, I'm sorry this happened. I know that we've had our differences in the past, but I have never hated you." Squeezing her hand, she continues to speak. "I have to admit that I've been pretty mad at you in the past, but I want you to know that nothing would make me happier than to see you and the baby well right now."

As Van stands at the bedside of Tee, she knows that it could have easily been her lying there. After hearing the tape on Tee's answering machine, she knows the attackers are looking for the tapes. She vows to herself, while still holding Tee's hand, to make everyone involved pay.

Q shakes June, Tim, and the rest of The Crew awake. Now all the guys sit in the lobby, each one with vengeful hearts.

Everyone sits and listens as Tim vents his frustration. "Whoever did this is heartless, homie. Tee is innocent, man. She didn't deserve any of this shit Q."

Q looks over at the whole Crew. All of them look at Tee as their Big Sis', so naturally they are upset. But looking at their faces now, upset is an understatement. They have death in their eyes. Knowing he could never keep the peace by telling them who is responsible, Q chooses to keep most of The Crew in the dark.

After everyone has spoken, he pulls June and Tim to the side. "Look homies, I want to pull your coat on something."

"What's poppin'," June says.

"Follow me," says Q.

They exit the hospital and stand outside of Q's car. He reaches inside the glove compartment and removes an adapter plug. He connects it to his cigarette lighter. Neither Tim nor June speak as Q pushes play on Tee's phone. Both shed tears as they hear Tee screaming for her life.

Q drops the machine back into his seat and turns and faces his homies. "Hope that after all this is over, we can all sit down and discuss each and every member of The Crew's future. This hustle game has taken some special people from our lives. We lost Umar. Then almost lost you," he says, putting his hand on Tim's shoulder.

"Now look at this. There is no way I'm gonna let these people who did this to Tee live. But what I'm saying to the both of you is this... You both have beautiful people in your lives, and The Game is dead. Get out while you still can homies. The reason why I'm saying this to you is because the rest of The Crew looks up to both of you. If you love them...

I mean really love them, then save them from 'The Belly of the Beast' prison, or worse, death and destruction."

———

JACOBS' FACE IS A MESS. TO COVER UP THE ATTACK, HE PURPOSELY lost control of his car a little less than a mile from his home. He is taken to the local hospital for a full report. Not only does he have an alibi, he has an excuse for why his face looks the way it does.

Sitting in his office, Jacobs holds a small mirror in front of his face. The black and blue swelling brings a slight chill over his body. He is no longer angry, but afraid. Afraid for his family. It doesn't matter that his parents are both ninety years old or his wife and kids have nothing to do with this whole thing. No, it doesn't matter. He had beaten and raped a very well respected woman beyond recognition. A woman who is an acquaintance of one of the most notorious drug lords in Rockingham, NC.

"Damn," Jacobs mumbles to himself, barely above a whisper. His thoughts turn to Tech. He hadn't heard from him since the attack. Tech left the salon at a dead run, never looking back. Jacobs knows Tech will eventually have to be put to sleep. He is their informant, but he can just as easily become someone else's.

Beep... Beep... Beep... Q's phone is sounding for the third time. He erases the number for the second time because it's an unfamiliar one. Today, he will be heading to the hospital. Tee is having her bandages removed. She seems calm, but Q knows she is worried. Beep... The phone sounds off again. Looking at the code behind the text makes Q run off the shoulder of the road.

"Shit," he says to himself as he regains control of the Corvette's wheels. "What is Asia calling me like this for? I told her I would call her back when I had time."

Q walks in Tee's room to find it occupied by several doctors and nurses. Most of whom are gathered around her bed. One doctor whispers a few comforting words in her ear as another begins removing the bandages. Tee is a nervous wreck. Her whole body trembles as the last bandages are removed. She doesn't know what to expect or take from the doctor's reaction, so naturally, she thinks the worst and starts to cry until one of the nurses holds a small mirror in front of her.

Her face bears no visible scars. She is speechless. The doctor in charge of the operation stands and admires his own work. All the commotion forces Q to her bedside. When she turns to face him, he can't believe his eyes. No scars, nothing!

Standing next to her, he did what he'd been waiting to do for weeks. He kisses her soft lips, savoring her taste. "You're beautiful ma," he says. "And I'm sor..."

"Shhh," Tee says, putting a finger to his lips. "I'm not going anywhere and leaving you and our son here," she says with a serious look in her eyes. She realizes she just told Q about the baby. "Q, did you hear what I said?"

"Yes ma, I heard you, and I'm not going to let you leave me and our son alone."

It's late in the afternoon when Q leaves the hospital. He is relieved to know that Tee's surgery had gone well and that the baby is fine. Even though the scars are not there physically, Q knows they are there mentally.

During their conversations, Tee could tell his mind was somewhere else. She knows that it is zero tolerance when it comes to people who Q loves, but this is worse. Her life has been put on the line. But she can't bear the thought of any children and women being hurt. Especially now that she is expecting a child herself. She knows she has to call Q and ask him to honor her request. He agrees with the first one. Tee knows she is stretching it with her last request. "No women either?" she asks.

Q gets quiet before he speaks. "But what about you Tee? You're a woman. What about our child? They didn't care about that!"

"Yes, I know," she says. "But you're not like them Q. Please, please Q"

He doesn't want to hang up on a sour note. So he agrees to honor both requests. As soon as he hangs up with Tee, the phone rings again.

"Damn, there is Asia ass again" Q thinks to himself. "Let me see what this girl want, she been hitting a nigga all day. He put his phone on speaker and dialed Asia's number. "Whatz up Asia?"

"Damn baby what took you so long to call me back, I need to ask you something important."

"What is it lady?"

"Well, Baby I really need your help. I just found out that my Pell grant check didn't go through, and I won't be able to graduate if I can't pay for this last semester."

"How much you need?"

"$15,000.00"

"When you need it?"

"By next Monday."

"Ok don't worry I got you"

"Thank you baby! Thank you! You know I'm going to do something extra special for you. Oh, one more thing, do you think you could drive me to Charlotte to pay for it."

"Yea, no problem, that way I can collect on that extra special thing coming my way."

Chapter Thirty-Five

The Hair Show

Elbony and Terri reopen the salon. Today the lobby is crowded. The main topic... gossip. They are still excited about the announcement Elbony made almost an hour ago. They were told that the hair show would be the following week. Q convinced the girls to have the show. He knew that Tee would have wanted it that way.

The shop is immaculate. The cleaning company always keeps the salon spotless, but no amount of cleaning can take away the pain Q feels whenever he enters Tee's office. As he sits in her office chair, his thoughts turn to Jacobs. Suddenly, an idea crosses his mind. Quickly, he picks up the phone and dials Attorney Wright's number. His secretary answers then puts him through.

"Yes, how can I help you?" says Wright.

"Mr. Wright, this is Q. Would it be alright if I stopped by the office?"

"I'll be waiting for your arrival," says Wright.

He really didn't have any real plans for Jacobs at this point, but with the news he'd given the attorney, Q hoped he would make his own plans. Plans to hold court in the streets.

The following week, the hair show is beautiful. Salons from all over are there showcasing different hair styles. Everybody is in attendance.

Terri and Elbony have put together a great show that will undoubtedly be talked about for the rest of the year.

Spotting June in the crowd, Elbony grabs his arm. "Hey Lil' brother. Is Q here yet?" she asks.

"Nah sis," he answers. "But they should be here soon.

"Okay. Let me know as soon as they arrive," she says.

"Aight sis."

Q pulls in first with Van following close behind. He gets out of the car and walks to Van's. Before he reaches the passenger's side, Tee is already in tears.

Q says, "Looks like they did a good job, huh." Tee nods in agreement.

"Come on, let's surprise everybody."

When Tee steps out of the car, she looks stunning. Her pregnancy is beginning to show. The whispers throughout the crowd suddenly become cheers.

"What's all the commotion?" El asks Terri while trying to see over the crowd.

"I don't know," says Terri.

As the crowd parts, they get their first look at Tee, who looks like magic walking towards them. They both run to their friend with open arms. As Q looks around the crowd, he doesn't see a dry eye in the building.

"You guys did a good job," says Tee. "I couldn't have done it any better myself. I'm proud of you both."

The hair show is a success with people already talking about next year. Q sits at the table alone watching the crowd. He is indeed a lucky man. Out of a terrible situation he has been blessed. His whole family is there and together. He never thought the day would come when Van and Tee would be side by side. But the news of the new baby has brought all things together. Hell, Van has already been out shopping for the baby's bedroom set and has informed Tee she would be by her side all the way through.

Chapter Thirty-Six

Truth Is Harder Than a Lie

That Monday, Q meets up with Asia to take her up to Charlotte to pay her tuition. On the way up, Asia is acting a little funny, but Q brushes it off. Maybe she isn't an early bird. Hell, he isn't used to being up this early in the morning either.

"Q when we get to Charlotte, can we stop and get something to eat before we pay the bill?" Asia asks.

"Yea, that's cool. What are you in the mood for?"

"Let's go to the IHop on Harris. I want some of those strawberry waffles."

"The IHop is cool, but why not go to the one on Independence since we already on this side?"

"They don't have turkey sausage, and you know you don't like me eating pork around you."

"True, true. I told you to stop eating that shit period though, that hog will have your skin all fucked up."

"Ok, ok. Don't start that Muslim stuff."

"That ain't no Muslim stuff, that's just some good shit a nigga trying to put you up on."

"Alright, so can we go to the one on Harris then?"

"Fo sho," Q replies.

When they pull into the IHop parking lot, it is packed even at 8:00 in the morning. Q drives around for what seems like an hour before he finally finds an empty spot. He follows a true OG move and backs his new pearl white jag into the open space.

As Q is about to exit the car, Asia blurts out, "Oh, I need to get the money from you."

"Damn! You can't wait until we come back to the car?"

"No, Baby. I want to put it in my pocketbook. That way, I will already have it when we get to the school."

"Alright, damn," Q says, looking at Asia as if she is crazy. He reaches into his glove box and gives Asia the money. She immediately begins to count it.

"Yo, Shawty! What you trying to do, get us robbed or something?"

"No, I'm sorry Babe. I just wanted to make sure it is all there."

"A nigga know how to count," Q says jokingly.

Asia puts the money in her purse and they proceed inside and sit down. Asia is busy choking down her food while Q is busy checking out the Dominican hostess that seated them. She has long black hair and a phat ass. Her face is so beautiful that he is trying to find a flaw. Unable too, Q is trying to figure out how he is going to crack on her without Asia knowing. Asia seems to be so preoccupied by the way she kept looking at her watch that it wouldn't be that difficult.

"Damn! You acting like you late for an important meeting or something."

"Naw, I just realized I left my phone in the car. I will be right back."

"Girl, quit tripping. We almost done. Whoever trying to call you can wait 10 more minutes." Then, Q realizes this could be his chance to holla at that Dominican princess and egg her on.

"Yea maybe you better go 'head and get your phone. I don't want you to miss your call. I will pay the bill and be right out." Q hands Asia the keys and when he is sure she is out of sight, he makes his way over to the hostess.

"Excuse me Adre...Adrianna," Q says trying to pronounce the name on the name tag.

"It's Adrianna," the woman responds.

"Yea Adrianna. Well Adrianna, I want to know what fool got a beautiful woman like you up in here working around pancakes. You need to be at home having someone bring you pancakes and whatever else you want."

"Oh is that so?"

"Yes, definitely so," Q says with a smile. "Look here's my number, call me if you want to change your life" Q writes his number down and pays the bill.

He walks outside to find Asia talking to some guy. Q gives the strange man the once over. By the way the man is dressed, he looks like a 50cent wannabe. He has on the whole NY hat and do rag, with the Timbs and all. Yea, this dude is definitely from New York. When Q hears his voice, it is confirmed. Q figures he is just some cat trying to holla. Hell, he has to admit Asia is looking good. *Funny how someone else tryin' to holla to remind you of what you already got,* Q thinks to himself as he approaches them.

Asia turns to him and introduces the New York strange. "Q this Tyreek, Tyreek this is Q."

"What up fam?" Both men talk as they dap one another up.

Behind him, Q could hear tire's screeching and siren's going. The next sound is police and federal agents yelling, "Get Down, everyone get down! get down on the ground!"

Q knows at that moment, he is being set up. He just doesn't know by whom and how. All the little things Asia has done begin to play back into his mind. Why didn't he trust his intuition?"

While he is being arrested in Charlotte, the rest of The Crew is being rounded up back in Rockingham. Once he is taken to the Mecklenburg County Jail and booked on conspiracy charges, the federal agents tell him how everything is about to play out.

"Man, you must have really pissed some people off," one agent replies. "The state handed us your case on a silver platter with a state witness to go along."

"Yeah, it doesn't get any easier," the old gray headed white agent agrees.

Q learns that Asia had told the feds he had her buying the dope for him from the New York nigga. That's why she needed Q to hand her the money. She had to make sure the Feds were able to see him reaching for the cash. She also had them dap up to show the completion of the deal. Asia had already put 2 kilos of cocaine in Q's car. She really done a job on the man she loves and would supposedly die for. He later finds out Asia had agreed to help the Feds after being approached by state agents, who had informed her that she would never practice law in North Carolina after being a known associate of a drug kingpin. Not willing to give up her future, she agreed to help them bring down Q.

When it comes down to it, Asia is only going to be there for Q if it doesn't mean harming herself. All Q can do is laugh. He knows that all this is bullshit, but he also knows that a lie is harder to disprove than the truth is to prove. In fact, these people don't care about the truth. They had what they wanted, him.

The news of Q's bust makes it back to Rockingham and is the talk of the town. When the media is through with the story, you would have thought he's Pablo Escobar.

ALL THE GIRLS GATHER AT THE SALON. VAN AND KIKI ARE ON THE way. As soon as Van walks in, she takes control of the situation. There isn't a dry eye in the building, and she doesn't like it.

She says to the girls, "What did I walk into, huh? A funeral? Look, you bitches better soldier tha' fuck up! Each and every one of them niggas have all of our backs. Now, it's time we have theirs. What would they think if they were to walk in and see us all puffy eyed and shit, when we're supposed to be out there picking up that money that we all know they left out in them streets? This is the best time for someone to try and get ghost on our people. And we not having that shit!"

Looking around the room, Van finally locks eyes with Tee who, as she expected, had not shed a tear, only because they had been schooled by the same man. They stare at each other for a moment before Van turns to leave.

Stopping at the door, she turns and says again, "Everybody keep your cell phones on and the lines free... I'll be in touch." With that she steps out of the office with Kiki by her side.

The End

The Crew's freedom? Find out in the sequel: Country Boys II - The Aftermath.
This will be the girl's time to shine!

Acknowledgments - Alan Little

This book is dedicated to the loving memory of my mother and father, Laura Jane Little, and Henry Lee Little.

Mom,
Through every trial and tribulation me and my siblings had to endure, you and Daddy were there. No hesitations, nothing but a mother and father's love. Even before your death, I remember the preparations you made to comfort us in our mourning. Even though you tried to ease the pain Mama, your presence was rooted too deep not to miss you every minute of the day. The hardest part for me was not being able to be there to say goodbye. Your words of encouragement and God's grace and mercy got me through. The peace that you have is the peace that I long for.

Dad,
You've only been gone a couple of months now, but it seems like forever. you will always be my best friend, hero, and arguably the best father who ever lived. I love you both and I will mourn you until I join you.

Baby Boy.
To my siblings, thank you for everything that you do.
My four beautiful children, Kiki, A.J, Zach, and D'undre, and to my goddaughter Melia Stevenson. I am so proud of all of you. Keep striving for greatness. DADDY'S LOVE.

Special dedication

Luvania, what up ma? I saved you for last for a lot of reasons. But you being last in my life is not one of them. Through everything, you showed me nothing but genuine love. I've made many mistakes in my life that stand to be corrected. Instead of correcting me on the spot, you have my back, knowing I am wrong. Then, you don't hesitate to check me in our privacy. I'm grateful for everything Van, especially your love. BULLETPROOF!

To my PlayTy familyTyrell, Elizabeth, and James,
We started this journey together, and every obstacle we've faced seemed to strengthen our bond even more. Thank you, Elizabeth, for your grittiness and diehard work ethic. James for your excellent camera work and masterful cover designs. Tyrell, your business mind is the glue my brother. Greatness!

A special shout out and thank you to everyone for their support, especially my city Rockingham, Hamlet, and all the surrounding counties. There are too many people to name, but know this, I genuinely appreciate ALL of you. Much love!

Other Books By Authors

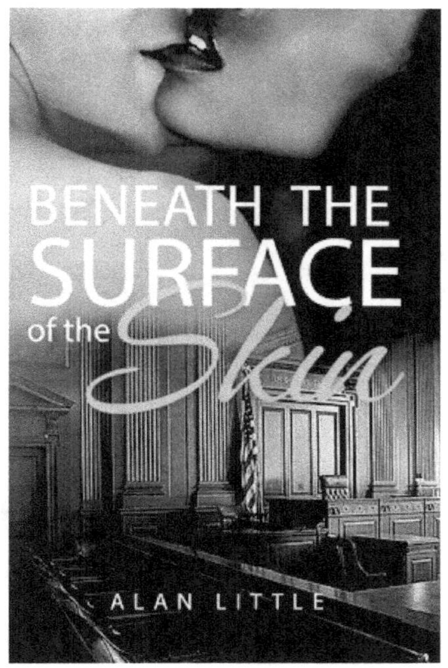

Beneath The Surface of the Skin

by Alan Little

About Author Alan Little

Born to a beautiful mother and father in the small city of Rockingham N.C. Alan was raised with five amazing siblings. Alan Little has created very successful waves throughout the urban- fiction community with titles such Country Boy I True Revenge I, True Revenge II, and Beneath the Surface.

Besides the title of best-selling author, Mr. Little's credentials also include the position of Talent Acquisition with PlaTy Multimedia and Publishing.

He is pleased to announce the re-release of his famed series, Country Boy. PlaTy Multimedia and Publishing will release the Country Boy series, along with a new final book in the series. Mr. Little stated, "It was an honor for PlaTy Multimedia and Publishing to be able to release the series and allow me to feel proud of some of my best works to date."

Although very passionate about his writing talent, Mr. Little spends a lot of his time with family, traveling, sports, and his forever need for speed, the drag strip.

www.ingramcontent.com/pod-product-compliance
Lightning Source LLC
Chambersburg PA
CBHW061308210726
48293CB00003B/1169